PRAISE FOR DANIEL PYLE

DISMEMBER

DISMEMBER'S *a fast-paced grindhouse-movie of a book with plenty of unexpected twists and turns and a fresh new crazy for a villain. The late Richard Laymon would have been grinning ear to ear.*

—JACK KETCHUM, author of THE GIRL NEXT DOOR

With DISMEMBER, *Daniel Pyle joins the select group of authors who can provide real chills and genuine surprises. Taut, weird, and intriguing.*

—JONATHAN MABERRY, author of GLIMPSE and INK

The tourniquet-tight plot and constant suspense keeps the pages flying. A solid, suspenseful thriller that enables readers to envision the movie it could become.

—PUBLISHERS WEEKLY

DOWN THE DRAIN

Pyle's tight little monster tale packs a nasty wallop.
—MICHAEL LOUIS CALVILLO,
author of *AS FATE WOULD HAVE IT*

Horror should be fun. Scary, of course...but above all, it should be fun. Too many people seem to have forgotten that. Well, Daniel Pyle has not forgotten. With his novella, DOWN THE DRAIN, Pyle has crafted a tale that evokes all the eye-popping strangeness and excitement that got me into horror in the first place. I loved it, and I can guarantee you'll never look at your bathtub the same again.
—JOE MCKINNEY, author of *DEAD CITY*

ALSO BY DANIEL PYLE

THE BUGS SULLIVAN SERIES
Breakdown

NOVELS
Dismember

NOVELLAS
Freeze
Down the Drain

COLLECTIONS
Advent

ANTHOLOGIES EDITED
Unnatural Disasters

DANIEL PYLE

Snowbirds

BLOOD BROTHERS PUBLISHING • 2024

Snowbirds first appeared in *Advent,*
copyright © 2022 by Daniel Pyle

Blood Brothers Publishing
www.bloodbrotherspublishing.com

ISBN: 978-0-9828691-2-3

1 3 5 7 9 11 10 8 6 4 2

For my brother, Samuel, as a partial apology
for that time I threw his LEGO set.

1

Liv sat alone on a park bench, studying the cluster of sky-scrapers towering over the distant trees. Her backpack lay on the ground between her feet, buzzing. She forced herself to ignore it, focusing instead on those gargantuan buildings, thinking about the thousands of people inside, wondering what kinds of problems *they'd* faced today.

In the snow-covered field beyond the bike path, a man pulled a toddler in an inflatable sled. Their breath wafted around their heads as they moved to a patch of untrampled powder, and the kid squealed when the man spun the sled in big, looping circles.

No problems for those two, it seemed. They appeared to be having the time of their lives. Although you could never really tell, could you? You never knew what heartache might be waiting elsewhere.

Liv shivered and tightened her scarf.

Somewhere, someone must be having a good day. A perfectly wonderful, absolutely terrific day.

But that person was not Liv.

Her backpack buzzed again, and she wrapped her arms around her stomach.

Fresh, lacy snowflakes seesawed down from the featureless

sky, decorating wool caps, thickening bare branches, covering the world. Liv knew she ought to get home before her parents started to worry...and before the weather had a chance to worsen.

And she would. Soon. But first she wanted to sit right here, thinking and trying not to, watching a happy kid in a colorful sled.

Her phone buzzed again, and she finally reached into her backpack to shut it off.

Then she cupped her face in her hands and bawled.

In the apartment, she stepped out of her wet boots and hung her backpack and outerwear on the coatrack behind the door.

Something smelled burnt, which meant her mom had decided to make dinner. Liv promised herself she wouldn't say anything.

When she stepped into the kitchen, she found Mom at the stove, biting her bottom lip and waving a towel over a baking dish filled with something as moist and colorful as a pile of charcoal.

Her dad sat at the dining room table, frowning at his laptop (aka working). His face looked stubblier than usual—verging on beardy—and based on the series of coffee rings wrinkling the stack of papers beside him, he was nursing what must have been his tenth cup. Which wasn't even close to a record.

"Hey, hon," he said, not looking up from his screen.

"Greetings from the land of showers and razors," she said.

"Har har."

Mom donned a pair of oven mitts and transferred the still-smoking dish to the sink.

"Sorry about dinner," she said. "I guess I forgot to set the timer."

Liv sat down at the table. "No prob. I can make myself a sandwich."

"Or," Mom said, "how about pizza?"

"Even better." Liv grabbed her dad's mug and sipped. "I hope there's whiskey in this."

Mom slapped her arm playfully as she joined them at the table.

"How was school?"

Liv shrugged. "I'd tell you, but I'm saving it for my memoirs." And before her mom could press further, she said, "How was work?"

Mom held her hand palm up and curled her fingers. Liv passed her the coffee.

"Hey, you little thieves," Dad said. "Make your own. That's the only thing keeping me alive."

Mom smiled, took her own sip, and handed the mug back to him. "Will it make me a bad parent if I say work sucked?"

"Not if it's true," Liv said. "And I guess we don't even need to ask Dad."

He pretended to smash his laptop, and they all laughed.

"Hey," Mom said, "there's something we wanted to ask you about." She looked at Dad, who lowered his screen and nodded.

"If it's about the birds and bees," Liv said, "I don't think you're old enough yet."

"We know all about that." Dad wiggled his eyebrows.

"Dad! Sick."

"You started it." He drained the last of his coffee and got up for a refill.

Liv turned to her mom and raised her eyebrows. "What's up?"

"How would you feel about spending Christmas in Florida?"

Liv glanced into the living room. Beside the sofa, their tree twinkled. "Florida?"

"With Nana."

Liv said nothing.

"I know how you love a white Christmas," Mom said, "but—"

"Is something wrong?"

"No." Dad had returned to the table. His coffee steamed. "Nothing's wrong. We just thought it might be nice to get away for a while."

Liv knew her parents had been going more than a little stir-crazy lately. They'd both been working from home for years, and they sometimes went literal weeks without even putting on their shoes, let alone leaving the apartment. She didn't blame them for wanting a change of scenery.

"But the thing is," Mom said, "we'd need to drive down, and we'd like to do that while we're both between work projects, which means leaving tomorrow. Can you do that? Miss next week? Any big tests or anything?"

It was Friday. Winter break didn't start until the following Thursday, but Liv knew for a fact that none of her teachers had anything important planned for the days leading up to then. Catch-up time for the slackers. Maybe some quasi-educational movies. Definitely plenty of goofing off.

"I have one last paper to finish," Liv said. "But I can do that tonight and email it to my teacher."

"You sure?" Mom said.

Liv nodded.

"So you're on board?" Dad said. "Christmas in the tropics?"

Liv didn't tell them the truth, that school was the last place she wanted to be, that the idea of walking the halls of Henry High gave her such anxiety it probably bordered on panic, or that she'd have spent the next three weeks cleaning bathrooms in a truck stop if it meant she didn't have to go back and face reality. Instead, she said, "I think that sounds awesome!"

Her parents looked at each other. They'd clearly expected more pushback.

"Well, okay then," Dad said. "It's a plan." He sipped from his mug. "Now, did I hear someone say *pizza*?"

After dinner, Liv curled up on the sofa with her tablet and added the final touches to her paper—some citations here, a conclusion there. She emailed it to her teacher with a short note letting him know about her trip and wishing him a happy Hanukkah. She did *not* check the rest of her messages.

Now free to officially forget about school and everything that went along with it, she did exactly that. She started a Christmas movie, wrapped her mom's favorite blanket around herself, and flopped back on the couch.

While the movie's opening credits rolled, she watched

multicolored lights race around their Christmas tree. She *would* miss spending the holiday at home (no sense denying that—to herself anyway), but regardless of anything else, the idea of visiting her grandma thrilled her. For most of her childhood, hardly a week had gone by without some quality Nana time, but since the move down south, Liv had seen her in person only half a dozen times or so. There'd been texts and calls and video chats, sure, but that wasn't the same, and they both knew it.

Better spend time with her while you still can.

Morbid, but true. She hoped her grandma still had plenty of Christmases left, but what if she didn't? Liv didn't want to think about it, but she also didn't want to *not* think about it. Because you couldn't prepare for something you never considered, right?

When the movie finally started, she shut her mind off for the first time that day and let herself enjoy it.

An hour later, her mom came in and asked if she'd packed.

Liv sucked air through her teeth. "I want to say yes."

"But?"

"But Mama didn't raise no liars." It was an old back-and-forth that made them both smile.

"Get to it," Mom said. "And then get some sleep. We're leaving at the crack of noon."

Liv gave her a mock salute.

"And don't *forget* your toothbrush," Mom said.

"Or what?"

"Or I'll wash your mouth out with soap."

Another back-and-forth. Another smile.

Liv retreated to her room and filled two duffle bags with clothes and other miscellaneous items she thought she might need or want. She considered taking her phone. Then she considered leaving it. Both options seemed ridiculous. She finally buried it in her sock drawer, satisfied it was the right decision. The only decision really.

Then she brushed her teeth, packed her toiletries, and got into bed. She lay there for a long time, staring at the ceiling, thinking about Christmas and her grandma, and trying with all her might not to think of anything else.

2

It took three trips for Liv and her parents to carry everything down to the parking garage. Dad, whose clean-shaven face made him look ten years younger (at least), loaded the suitcases and bags in the trunk first and then piled a layer of wrapped Christmas gifts on top while Mom situated their things in the front of the car.

"Okay," Dad said and slammed the lid, "let's hit the road!"

Liv held out her hand. "I'll drive."

Dad laughed. "Dream on."

"Come on." She gave him her best pout. "I'm serious. What's the point of getting my license if I never get to drive anywhere?"

"You're driving me insane," Dad said. "Does that count?"

Liv crossed her arms. "Really? Dad jokes? This is no time for dad jokes."

"First of all," Dad said, "it's always time for dad jokes. Everybody knows that." He bounced the keys in his hand. "How about we let you drive for a while once we get out of the city?"

Mom had joined them at the back of the car. She'd pulled her hair back in a ponytail, and it emphasized a few new streaks of gray at her temples. Dad looked to her for confirmation, and she nodded reluctantly.

"Like on actual roads?" Liv said. "If you bring me to a supermarket parking lot again so I can practice parking, I'm gonna lose my spit."

"Honest-to-god roads," Dad said. "I spit you not."

They smiled at each other.

Mom rolled her eyes and said, "I can't believe I'm gonna be stuck in the car with you two for two and a half days."

"Better than being stuck in the apartment though, right?" Dad said.

She agreed. It *was* better.

They hadn't even left the building yet, but Liv could already taste the escape, and she knew they could too.

They clambered into the car, and Dad spun the radio's dial until he found a station playing Christmas music. As they pulled out of the garage and away from the building, their collective excitement grew downright palpable.

"Florida, here we come!" Dad said and honked the horn.

A green-haired kid carrying a skateboard jerked his head toward them, looking first scared and then annoyed. When he flipped them the bird, Liv returned the gesture with a friendly wave. He tilted his head quizzically, hopped on his board, and rolled away.

"Crank the volume," Liv said and smiled when the music filled the car.

That night, they stopped at a hotel just outside Clarksville, Tennessee. Mom had booked it in advance, and when they pulled up, she told them it had looked much nicer on the website.

"It'll be fine," Dad said with what sounded like total sincerity.

And Liv agreed. It had beds, and that was all she cared about. After being stuck in the car all day, she was ready for some serious sprawling and some even more serious snoozing.

While Mom checked them in, Dad parked the car. He and Liv grabbed their few overnight items.

"You did a good job today," Dad said.

They'd let her drive for almost an hour. There'd been highways and ramps, both off and on, and sections of six-lane traffic with merging semis, and Liv had handled it all like a pro. Despite one especially stressful exit that left her yearning to pull over and scream, she'd held it together, and she was proud of herself. When they finally stopped to gas up and switch drivers, she didn't think she'd ever felt more grown up.

"Thanks," she said.

"And I don't just mean with the driving." He adjusted the strap of a crossbody bag and led her toward the hotel.

"Huh?"

"The whole thing," he said. "All that time in the car. Agreeing to go on the trip in the first place and spend your Christmas away from home. I appreciate it. We both do."

"It's no biggie," she said. "I mean, we're *all* spending Christmas away from home, right? But it's not like we're going off to war or something. And I'm excited to see Nana."

He told her he was too, and they stepped into the lobby.

In the middle of the night, Liv woke to the sound of whispering.

She'd been too tired to shower or even brush her teeth and had crawled under her blankets and fallen asleep within minutes of entering their room. Now, twisted up in unfamiliar sheets and wedged between two piles of discount pillows, she felt sweaty and disoriented. Her tongue darted around her mouth like a fish in a toilet.

The whispering continued.

Liv couldn't make out what her parents were saying, but she thought she heard her name more than once. She opened one eye and looked toward their bed, but with the curtains closed, the room was almost completely dark. An alarm clock on the table between their beds provided just enough ghostly light to give the two lumps in the other bed some vague definition.

Were they talking about her? In the middle of the night? And if so, why?

She scooted across her mattress, trying to get just a few inches closer.

One of her pillows flopped off the bed and struck the floor with a gentle *plop*.

"Liv?" Her mom sounded both surprised and a little...what...guilty maybe?

"Mmmmmhmmm," she said, trying to sound less awake than she really was.

"Get some sleep," Mom said. "We've got another long day on the road tomorrow."

"K." She reached over the edge of the bed and retrieved the pillow.

"Love you."

"Love you too," Liv said.

She waited for a while before allowing herself to drift off again. There was no more whispering.

3

Earlier that evening, Darrel sat in his parked car with the window rolled down and breathed in the fresh, warm Florida air. Could this seriously be December? If not for the scattering of Christmas lights up and down the street, he never would have believed the holiday was only weeks away.

No wonder so many people chose to spend their golden years down here.

He leaned back, took another deep breath, and turned to look at the small bungalow he'd just departed. He imagined his mom in there, sitting at the table where he'd left her with her cookies and that foul-smelling tea she loved so much.

Should he have helped her get ready for bed?

No, of course not. She wasn't one of those feeble, helpless geezers. An offer like that would have hurt her pride. Never mind that she'd spent his entire childhood putting him to bed. Never mind that he'd have been perfectly happy to return the favor.

Someday soon, pride might no longer be a factor, and if (when) that day came, he promised himself he'd be there for her.

Whether she liked it or not.

He stuck his key in the ignition, but before he turned it,

he saw movement from the corner of his eye and turned back toward the bungalow.

A dark shape, just a shadow really, darted from the front stoop to the bushes beneath the bedroom window.

Except that was silly, wasn't it? Surely it had been a trick of the light, a bird flying past a streetlamp or a cloud sliding through the moonlight.

He leaned over the passenger seat, squinting.

The shape moved again, standing this time. Against the lit window, its head was nothing but a black blur. It swayed from side to side. Then it dropped again and scurried toward the corner of the house.

Darrel jumped out of the car and ran up the front walkway, dialing 911 as he scanned the area.

The Florida air, so alluring only moments ago, felt thicker now. Stifling. His heart slapped his ribs, and he tried not to hyperventilate.

When the operator came on the line and asked about his emergency, he explained the situation while fumbling for the flashlight function on his phone. He found it, put the phone on speaker, and held it out in front of himself, illuminating the minuscule yard.

The operator asked another question, and he had to ask her to repeat it. He found it almost impossible to focus on her voice.

"Does this person have a weapon?" she said. "A gun or a knife or anything like that?"

"No," Darrel whispered. "I mean, I don't know. I couldn't tell. It's dark."

His light swept from left to right, right to left. He took another step forward.

"We have a unit on the way," the operator said. "Are you somewhere safe?"

Something sloshed around the side of the bungalow. It sounded like someone rocking a rain barrel. Instead of responding to the operator, he took another step toward the noise.

"Hello?" he said.

"I'm here, sir," the operator said.

"No, not you."

The sloshing stopped, leaving only the sounds of distant traffic and his thumping chest.

He inched forward, still holding the phone at arm's length.

When something flicked out of the shadows and knocked the phone from his hand, he screamed.

The phone tumbled across the yard and landed face up, flashlight down.

The operator said, "Sir, are you all right?"

Darrel was not all right.

The dark shape dragged him into the shadows, and his screaming first intensified, and then slowed, and then stopped. The sound that replaced it was the hurried chewing and slurping of something desperately hungry.

4

"You did what?"

They'd made it out of Atlanta not long ago and were now cruising through a less-frantic stretch of rural land.

"I left it at home," Liv said. She marked her place in the paperback she'd been reading and dropped the book onto the seat beside her.

Mom turned around, straining against her seat belt. "We can't go back now," she said. "I asked you a hundred times if you had everything."

"I don't want to go back," Liv said. "And I do have everything."

"What do you mean?" Dad peeked at her in the rearview mirror. "You left it on purpose?"

Liv nodded.

"Why?" Mom said, really fighting the belt now.

Liv bit her bottom lip. "I just...didn't want the distraction." It was the only way she could think to say it that wasn't a flat-out lie.

"Well that was stupid," Mom said.

"Hey," Dad said, "easy."

"Don't *easy* me. It was stupid. What if we get separated? What if we need to get ahold of you?"

Liv frowned. It genuinely hadn't occurred to her to talk the whole phone thing over with them. It wasn't like they were anti-technology freaks—working from home, they spent the majority of their time staring at one screen or another—but if anything, she'd have thought they'd be excited about a trip where they could have as much of her attention as they wanted. "How would we get separated? We're six inches apart."

"You know what I mean," Mom said.

Actually, Liv didn't.

"We won't be together every second of every day. I need to be able to reach you."

"People existed for hundreds of thousands of years without phones," Liv said.

Mom faced front and leaned back against her seat with a huff.

"But I am sorry," Liv said. "I seriously didn't mean to cause trouble or anything. I didn't think about it."

A mud-splattered van passed them on the left. A little boy with a rat's nest of blond hair pressed his mouth against his window and made a silly face as they went by. Liv smiled at him.

"It's okay," Dad said. "We'll pick up a burner phone when we get down there." He looked at her in the mirror again and then at Mom. "Problem solved?"

A prepaid phone was fine with Liv. No one besides her parents would have the number, so it wouldn't be anything she'd need to constantly worry about. She agreed.

Dad turned to Mom. She told him that sounded fine and apologized for losing her temper.

"It's okay," Liv said. "I think you've gotta expect some

short tempers when you've spent two days in a big metal box full of Dad's farts."

They all laughed. Then Dad reminded her that some of those farts had been hers as well, and they laughed even harder.

After things quieted down again, Liv picked up her book, found her place, and continued to read.

They stayed near Ocala that night. It was only two more hours to their final destination, and if they'd known that day's drive would be such an easy one, they might have driven straight through and skipped the second hotel altogether, but you could never really predict something like that, could you? They'd wanted to give themselves plenty of cushion in case they had a flat tire or ran out of gas or...well, whatever, so Mom hadn't scheduled their reservation at the resort to start until the following day, and it was too late to change it now.

But that was fine. This way, they could show up fresh faced the next morning, ready to enjoy their first full, real day of vacation.

They reached the hotel just before midnight and piled out of the car.

Ocala wasn't much better than Clarksville, but, again, it didn't need to be.

Liv fell onto her bed and drifted off almost immediately. If there were more late-night whispers, she slept right through them.

She dreamed she was running down a beach. Running and running and running. But she wasn't sure whether she was running away from something...or something was running away from her.

When they reached White Beach around lunchtime the next day, they stopped at their hotel first.

It was a lavish, sprawling resort right on the Gulf of Mexico, surrounded by palm trees and sparkling pools. Liv hadn't thought to ask where they'd be staying, and she definitely hadn't expected this.

When they circled the building, she spotted a group of children splashing one another at the shallow end of one of the pools. A pair of women watched from nearby lounge chairs, waving when the kids called to them. Liv heard the children's giggles through the car windows.

They drove between beautifully landscaped beds of lush, exotic flowers and perfectly manicured hedges as they approached the resort's grand main entrance.

Dad whistled. "This place is amazing."

Liv agreed.

"How can we afford this?" Dad asked.

"It was a last-minute booking," Mom said. "Maybe a cancellation they needed to fill or something. I don't know. It was actually one of the cheapest options I could find. I knew it was a good deal, but I didn't realize it was *this* good."

A valet opened their doors for them, and a bellhop loaded their luggage onto a cart.

"This must be what it feels like to be a king," Dad said.

Liv nodded. "Or a rock star."

Dad said, "Or the king of rock and roll," and did a little Elvis dance move.

"Okay," Liv said, "you win. Just promise you'll never do that again."

Dad wrapped his arm around Liv's shoulders, gave her a squeeze, and told her he made no such promises.

"I'm sorry," Mom told the valet. "They think they're funny."

"Everyone's funny at The Beachside Resort," the man said. He had a very faint accent. Cuban maybe. When he smiled, he revealed what must have been the two most perfect rows of teeth Liv had ever seen.

"I give them one star for creative naming," Dad said. "But five out of five for everything else."

He handed the car keys and a tip to the valet. Then they all followed the bellhop into the lobby.

An enormous Christmas tree filled the far end of the entryway. An array of ornaments in various shades of silver and blue covered its branches, and what must have been dozens of strands of lights twinkled within its depths. Lengths of garland sporting tinsel and silver bells edged the ceiling, a wooden table with complimentary cucumber water and cookies, and the elegant front desk. It was just enough decoration to be festive but not gaudy, Liv decided after taking it all in. But it was also more than a little disorienting—it was easy to forget what time of year it was when there were tropical flowers and pools full of splashing kids outside. It felt like they'd traveled through time.

The bellhop led them to the front desk, where a beautiful woman in a shimmering blouse welcomed them warmly.

Their room—if you could call it that—had a full kitchen, a living room with a TV the size of a small country, and two separate bedrooms. A glass door led onto a balcony that overlooked a gorgeous beach three stories down and the gulf beyond. The air was full of the sounds of happy tourists and squawking seagulls.

"This really is unbelievable," Mom said. "I've never stayed anywhere this nice. Not even close."

"I've never even *lived* anywhere this nice," Dad said.

Liv thought he'd meant it as a joke, but she couldn't be sure. This was definitely nicer than their apartment, and that was the only place she'd ever lived.

The bellhop unloaded their luggage by the door before wishing them a wonderful stay and heading off to his next task. Liv grabbed her bags from beside the pile of Christmas presents and took them to her room.

Her bed was an expansive joke of a thing that wouldn't have fit in her room back home, and she had her own TV, though hers was much more reasonably sized. The room smelled sweet, flowery, and clean, and the window gave her another beautiful view of the water. Liv dropped her bags on the bed and poked her head through the room's second door.

Her own bathroom!

It wasn't huge, but it had everything she'd need, including a shower with fancy dual shower heads.

She'd never had her own bathroom before. Even on vacation. The idea of it was more than exciting—it was downright mind-blowing.

In the other room, her mom screeched, and Liv ran out to see what was going on.

She found her parents standing in front of their own bathroom door, mouths agape.

Mom turned to her. "We have a hot tub," she said. "A hot tub *in the room*."

Liv laughed and peeked between them. Their bathroom was bigger than hers, and it did, in fact, have a hot tub. "It's a Christmas miracle," she said and leaned her head against her mom's arm.

"I call first dibs," Dad said.

"Oh no you don't." Mom pushed him playfully away from the bathroom door. "Ladies first."

After one last appreciative glance at the bathroom, they all went out to enjoy the view from the deck.

"They call this winter?" Dad said after they spotted a couple of shirtless boys tossing a football back and forth on the beach.

"More like late, late summer," Liv said, "leading straight into early, early next summer."

A seagull soared down toward the gulf, gliding motionlessly and reminding Liv of a paper airplane.

"I'm so glad we did this," Mom said.

Dad and Liv agreed.

Liv still wasn't sure how she felt about waking on Christmas morning to the sounds of crashing waves, but life was all about new experiences, right? And she knew this was one she'd never forget.

"Later," Dad said, "we'll find a grocery store and stock the fridge, but first…"

"Nana?" Liv clutched her hands together and bounced. "Nana!"

5

Connie tied off her thread and held the last of the stockings at arm's length to inspect her work.

Livinia's name ran across the top cuff in swooping red letters. It wasn't perfect, but nothing handmade ever was. Connie was a staunch believer in the charm of imperfection.

She placed the stocking on her little kitchen table beside the ones she'd already finished for Benji and Em. *Benjamin* and *Emily*. Always full names for stockings—her mother had taught her that. She'd used an adorable snowman fabric for Liv's, and though she thought it might be too cutesy for a sixteen-year-old, she hoped it would remind her granddaughter that Christmas was all about bringing out the child in all of us.

Steam drifted up from a coffee mug on the corner of the table, and she took a sip before carrying the stockings into the living room.

The cottage didn't have a fireplace (who needed one down here?), but it did have a faux mantel on the wall below the TV. She hung the stockings from a series of brass holders that had seen nearly a hundred Christmases. She knew they already had stockings of their own—she'd made Benji's herself all those years ago—but she wasn't sure they'd remember to bring them, and she wanted to be sure they all felt welcome and loved. They were coming all the way down here to be with her after all. It was the least she could do.

Her own stocking hung next to theirs. It had frayed edges and a few stains she hadn't been able to remove, and though a less sentimental person might have tossed it long ago, she would never get rid of it. Her mother had made it over sixty-five years ago. It had been there in Connie's small childhood home, hanging from the fireplace by her daddy's reading chair every Christmas, in the much bigger house where she and Henry had raised the boys, and now here, in her cozy cottage, most likely the last place she'd ever call home. *Constance*, it read in faded green thread.

The tree occupied a corner on the other side of the room, next to her own reading chair. It was humble and artificial, but she'd filled it with ornaments dating all the way back to her grandmother's time. There was the wooden snowman her father had carved, a hand-painted Santa Benji had made her in his kindergarten art class, and so many more. Each decoration brought back its own special memory: the smell of wood shavings on her father's shirt and Benji's proud, gap-toothed smile. She inevitably teared up when it came time to decorate the tree, but they were *good* tears.

She turned her attention back to the mantel, adjusted the stockings until they looked evenly spaced—or close enough—and returned to the kitchen for her coffee.

When the doorbell rang, she'd just pulled a pan of fresh cookies from the oven—gingerbread men, Benji's favorite—and though they were slightly more done than she would have liked, they still looked and smelled delicious. She placed the pan on the stovetop, flopped the oven mitts down beside it, and hurried to the front door.

Liv burst inside first, tall and more beautiful than ever. Connie knew the girl had some of her genes somewhere deep inside her, but the surface layer was all Em. The two could have been sisters, and Connie knew people often mistook them for such. Liv wrapped her arms around Connie and gave her a good hug.

"Nana!" she said. "I've missed you so much."

"Me too," she said, ignoring the dull, ever-present arthritic pain in her wrists and hugging back with all the strength she could muster.

Em came next, and Connie hugged her just as hard. As far as Connie was concerned, Em was as much her child as the ones she'd given birth to. Em squeezed her, gave her a kiss on the cheek, and told her the place smelled delicious.

"It's gingerbread dudes!" Benji said. His boyhood name for the cookies. He approached Connie, and she held her hands out.

"My boy."

They hugged for a long time, as if it had been years since they'd seen each other instead of only months.

"Hey, Mom," Benji said and pinched her earlobe. It was a silly family tradition that had become an unbreakable habit.

Liv crossed to the stove, leaned close to the cookies, closed her eyes, and took a deep whiff.

"Oh man," she said. "I want to bite one of their heads off so bad."

Liv might look like her mom, but her personality had always been pure Benji.

"I guess you found the place okay," Connie said. She'd lived here for several years, but when it came time for visits, she'd always been the one to do the traveling. Though they'd seen pictures and videos of her cottage, they'd never been here in person. Not that she begrudged them this, of course —it made much more sense, both practically and financially, for a single retired person to take a quick flight than it did for a working couple and their child to make a multi-day drive or spend a fortune on plane tickets.

"No problem at all," Em said. "The neighborhood's so nice. It seems perfect."

"It is," Connie agreed. "I love it here. How about I give you a tour of the house and then we massacre some ginger-bread dudes."

"Good lord," Em said. "Now there are three of you."

Connie chuckled.

"And you love it," Benji said. He gave Em a kiss on the forehead.

"Yeah," Em said, "I do actually. Which probably just means I have a brain tumor."

Doing their best Schwarzeneggers, Benji and Liv said, "It's not a tumor!" in perfect synchronization.

Em shook her head.

It didn't take more than a few minutes for Connie to show them around the place. As she led them from the eat-in kitchen to her bedroom, the bathroom, and the laundry alcove, she tried to see the place through their eyes. Though it was small, she thought she'd done a pretty good job of making it homey, and based on their cheerful compliments, they seemed to agree. When she showed them the living room, Liv spotted the stockings and ran over to examine hers more closely.

"You made us stockings," she said and grinned. "I love the snowmen!"

Which, of course, brought a big smile to Connie's face.

"You didn't have to do that," Benji said.

"I wasn't sure if you'd bring yours," Connie said, "and by the time I thought to ask, it was too late."

"We didn't," Em said. "It completely slipped my mind. Thank you."

Connie made a shooing motion. "It's no big deal."

"Yeah right," Benji said. "How many hours did you spend on those?" He gave Connie another hug. "Do I have the best mom or what?"

"Actually," Connie said, "I think Liv has the best mom."

Em gave her a look that said both *Thank you* and *We both know that's a load of BS.*

"Liv," Connie said. "Could you and your mom ice the cookies? The icing's bagged up in the fridge."

Benji gave her a knowing glance over the top of Liv's head.

"Sure," Liv said. She grabbed her mom's hand and led her into the kitchen.

Connie took Benji the other way, through the sliding glass door that led to the back patio, where they could have a quiet, private conversation.

6

Fred sat in a cheap plastic chair at the edge of the community-center auditorium, curling further and further into himself with each new word Dorothea screamed at him. Agnes stood by the refreshment table across the room, spooning grounds into the coffee maker and unboxing a batch of fresh doughnuts. Fred couldn't tell if she was trying to stay out of the argument or only waiting until Dorothea's fury waned before joining her in the tongue lashing.

"Do you not know how to read a calendar?" Dorothea said. "Or are you purposefully trying to ruin everything?" She was a tall woman with a long, thin nose that made her face look honed. If she looked directly at you, you got the impression you were staring at the cutting edge of a blade. When she spoke, her wrinkly neck wobbled, dulling some of that lethal quality, but not all of it.

Fred ran a hand through his wispy halo of hair. "I'm sorry," he said for the hundredth time.

"Did you learn nothing from Italy? We have a schedule for a reason. You're a year early, and now you've put everything in jeopardy again."

"I know," Fred said, "but..."

Across the room, Agnes turned to watch but said nothing.

"Let me guess," Dorothea said, "you're sorry?"

Fred huffed and slapped his legs. "Well, yes, I am. I didn't do it on purpose. You have no idea how he smelled...and how hungry I was. It was just instinct. I've been so hungry for so long."

"And we haven't?" Dorothea stomped and crossed her arms beneath her shallow bosom. "You think we don't have the same temptations?"

Fred hung his head.

"And worst of all," Dorothea said, "you left *evidence*. If you were going to do it, at least you could have brought him back to us. You could have *shared*, and they'd have nothing but their suspicions."

"But I didn't leave the body." He knew it was a stupid thing to say as soon as the words left his mouth.

"That. Doesn't. Matter."

Dorothea's mouth opened unnaturally wide with the last word, and Fred saw her eyes begin to darken and shift toward the sides of her head.

The coffee maker gurgled. Agnes walked away from the table and joined them. Her curls of bluish cotton-candy hair practically glowed beneath the room's fluorescent lights. "What does this mean for us?"

Dorothea shook her head, and her features snapped back to normal. She rubbed the bridge of her nose. "It means there's going to be twice the scrutiny there should have been. And before we're ready to deal with it. It means we'll have to move up our timetable and pray nothing worse happens." She glared at Fred.

"Move it up how far?" Agnes's pupils looked enormous behind her thick glasses, owl-like, but there was nothing out of control about that—those lenses had always distorted her eyes.

"There's no reason to wait any longer," Dorothea said. "Fred's looking younger already. People might start to notice."

Fred shifted uncomfortably in his chair. He'd studied himself intently in the bathroom mirror that morning. His liver spots were less dense than they had been just days ago. His hair, though still thin, was a distinctly darker shade of gray. His crow's feet had shallowed and shortened. No one would have looked him over and called him young, and it was unlikely anyone but Agnes and Dorothea would notice the subtle shift at all, but it wasn't *impossible.*

"We'll start tonight," Dorothea said.

Agnes nodded and walked back to the refreshment table.

"And if anyone says anything about how good you're looking," Dorothea told Fred, "you tell them—"

"I know," Fred said, "I know. I've been taking my vitamins. I'm sorry, Thea."

"You better be."

She took a pile of bingo cards from a nearby table and handed him half. "Help me put these out."

He stood (with nary a creaking joint to be heard) and took his share of the cards to the other end of the room.

Soon, hunched men and women began shuffling into the hall. Fred handed them daubers as they stepped in and motioned toward the waiting tables. The geezers smelled like spoiled meat, and as the room filled, the stench intensified. Fred couldn't unsmell it, but he could ignore it. He'd had lifetimes of practice.

7

Liv and her mom sat across the table from each other, giving the gingerbread dudes faces and rudimentary clothing. Between two cookies, Liv noticed Mom had stopped moving and looked up.

Mom watched her silently, one corner of her mouth turned up in a way that made her look like someone lost in a happy thought.

"Can I help you, creeper?"

Mom said, "I was just remembering a gingerbread house we made when you were a little girl. Do you remember that?"

"The one with the dinosaur?"

Mom laughed. "Yep."

In first grade, Liv's teacher sent her home with a bag full of leftover supplies from their holiday party. It had taken some serious begging, but Liv had finally convinced her parents to help her make her very own little house. When one of the house's walls caved in, Dad added a toy T-rex to the project and cracked some joke about Jurassic Park being a terrible place to build your house. Liv, who had been seconds away from a crying fit, came down with a serious case of the giggles instead, and they'd left the dino-wrecked structure in the middle of the dining room table like a decorative centerpiece all month.

"Hey," Mom said.

"Hmmm?" She'd gone back to her icing and was currently giving one of the cookies a surprised O for a mouth.

"What would you think about spending a night or two here with Nana?"

Liv licked icing from one of her knuckles. "All of us?"

Mom shook her head. "There isn't room for all of us, but we thought it might be fun for you."

Liv frowned and wondered if her mom thought she didn't see what was happening. Was she supposed to believe Dad and Nana had snuck off into the back yard to have some totally unrelated, mysterious conversation?

They'd clearly planned this whole thing beforehand. *We thought?* Not exactly a spur-of-the-moment idea.

So why act so weird about it? Why not tell her on the drive down? Or at the hotel? Or any other time? Why try to play it off as something spontaneous? They didn't need to trick her into spending time with her grandmother. It wasn't the only reason she'd been happy to make the trip, but it was the *main* reason.

"Sure," Liv said. "That would be cool."

"Just like that?"

Liv looked up again. "Is something going on?"

"What do you mean?" Mom picked up one of the un-iced cookies, bit off an arm, and chewed nervously.

"Are you and Dad...okay?"

Now Mom looked genuinely confused. "Me and Dad? What do you mean?"

"You're not getting a..." She couldn't look her mom in the eye and focused on the cookies instead. She started again: "You're not getting divorced or something, are you?"

Mom laughed, and Liv looked back up. Mom held the back of her hand up to her mouth to keep from spitting out cookie crumbs. "No, we aren't getting divorced. Why would you ask that?"

Liv shrugged.

"Do we not seem madly in love?"

"I don't know," Liv said. "I guess. But I don't spend all day with you. And..."

"What?"

"Parents hide things sometimes, right?"

To this, Mom said nothing.

"Nana isn't sick is she?"

"Jesus." Mom wiped her mouth and shook her head. "No, Nana's fine. There's nothing...nefarious going on. We just thought you'd like to have a sleepover. Like the old days."

"So why not just tell me earlier?" Liv said. "I'm *excited* to see Nana. Why all the...what do you call it?"

"Subterfuge?"

"Sure."

Mom hesitated a second. "I don't know," she said. "The resort is so much nicer than we expected, and I know you were excited about the bathroom and everything. I just want you to have a good time down here."

"I will," Liv said. "And I am excited about the hotel, but there will still be plenty of time for that. I'm more excited to spend time with Nana."

Mom grasped Liv's hand. "I'm sorry if I worried you. I didn't mean to."

Liv told her it was no big deal.

"You're a good kid. You know that?"

Liv said nothing. She didn't want to disagree. Not out loud.

After a few seconds, Mom withdrew her hand and they both continued icing.

They'd made a quick trip back to the resort for Liv's overnight bag before returning for an early dinner around Nana's kitchen table. Peanut butter and jelly sandwiches. Nothing but the finest cuisine at Nana's Gourmet Delicatessen.

They stayed at the table long after they'd finished eating, catching up and reminiscing, planning some of the particulars of the rest of their stay (Christmas morning here at the cottage, they'd all agreed, and a fancy steak dinner at a nearby restaurant Nana recommended sometime between now and then). When Mom and Dad finally said their goodbyes, they all traded a series of hugs.

"Be good," Liv said as they walked back toward the car.

"That's our line," Dad said and gave her a little wave.

After they'd gone, Liv plopped down on Nana's sofa and pulled out the prepaid phone they'd bought earlier at a ghost town of a strip mall. It looked and felt cheap, but it wasn't as old school as she'd expected. A touch screen—not a flip phone. She double-checked that she'd programmed both parents' numbers into it, sent them each a test text, and stuffed the phone back into her pocket.

Nana sat down beside her. "Now the real fun begins."

Liv smiled.

"What would you like to do?"

Liv pretended to think for a second. "How about some cocaine?"

"Sorry," Nana said, "this is a heroin household."

"Fine. I'll tie you off first."

Nana laughed. "Should I be worried that you seem to know so much about it?"

"Only from the movies," Liv said and held up two fingers in a V shape. "Scout's honor."

"That's the peace sign, you little liar."

They both smiled, and Nana gave Liv another hug. "I'm so happy you're here."

"Me too," Liv said.

"So what do you really want to do?"

Liv shrugged. "What do you normally do after dinner?"

"Sometimes I walk to the beach," Nana said. "It's only about four blocks away."

Liv sat up straight and slapped her hands together. "Yes! Can we do that? Please?"

"Of course. Just let me get my shoes."

Liv waited at the front door. She'd seen the gulf from their balcony at the resort, but she hadn't actually stepped foot on a beach since their trip to California ten years earlier. She imagined the feel of the sand between her bare toes, the smell of the salty water. When Nana joined her, she wore a thin windbreaker and a pair of tan shoes that matched the earpieces of her librarianesque glasses. Liv grinned, opened the door, and hurried through.

The weather outside was *not* frightful. Liv led Nana to the edge of her property, taking in the palm trees scattered around the neighborhood and the pinkening sky. She took a deep breath of warm, smogless air.

"I can see why you like it down here," Liv said.

Nana smiled. "Beautiful, isn't it?"

"Do you ever miss the snow?"

"My joints sure don't," Nana said.

"What about the rest of you?"

"Sometimes."

They moved down the sidewalk side by side and passed the house next door. It had a shallow porch with a pair of matching rocking chairs and potted ferns hanging from the soffit.

"You like your neighbors?"

Nana nodded and said in a whisper, "I like this one. Harriet. She and I play cards and have coffee sometimes. The woman the other way is a bit of a busybody."

"If I see her," Liv said, "I'll spit on her."

"Thank you."

"Aren't there any men?"

"Some," Nana said, "but there are more women. Life expectancies and all that."

"That's a bummer."

"Not for the surviving men."

They reached the corner, looked both ways, and crossed to the next block.

"Do you have a...what do the old people call it? A gentleman caller?"

"Just how old do you think I am?"

Liv smiled and brushed her hair out of her face.

"And in answer to your question, a lady never tells. How about you? Any gentlemen callers in your life?"

Liv hesitated only a second before saying, "A lady never tells."

"Ah, so wisdom *can* be passed down through the generations."

They continued down the street. It was no cookie-cutter neighborhood—each house had its own personality. Stucco here, brick there. Some had porches and others only stoops. There were lawn ornaments and welcome signs, picket fences and yapping dogs. Not to mention a healthy mixture of unique Christmas decorations. Liv knew it was technically some kind of retirement community, with dues and rules and a whole host of benefits—like people to mow your yard and access to the community pool and health center—but on the surface, it looked like any other neighborhood. Cleaner than the city back home for sure, and with houses maybe smaller than average, but nice and cozy, and full of character. Liv wasn't sure what she had expected. Not a prison exactly, but definitely something more depressing than this.

The one thing she couldn't get over was how *green* everything looked. She wondered how lush the place must be in the spring.

Another block down, they passed a small church with a well-worn nativity scene in the strip of grass between the sidewalk and the parking lot. Though the wooden manger and ceramic figures were well faded, they weren't dirty. Liv spotted not a single bird splat, despite the skyful of splatterers. Someone had been doing a terrific job of keeping the decorations presentable—maybe the same people who kept up everything else around here.

They rounded a curve in the road, and Liv spotted the beach ahead. When they reached it, she slipped her sneakers off and ran into the sand like a little kid, feeling freer than she had in years. She looked back, and Nana gave her a broad, happy smile.

Across the gulf, the sun bobbed on the horizon. A young couple sat shoulder to shoulder near the water's edge, kicking at the waves when they rolled over their bare feet. A trio of elderly men in fishing hats sat in folding chairs farther up the coast. One said something in a low, raspy voice, and the others chuckled. Liv rolled up her pants, walked into the surf until it reached halfway up her shins, and stared out across the water. Rays of sunshine flickered across the rippling surface like firelight. Liv stood there motionless until only a crescent of sun remained. Then she walked out of the water and joined her grandmother in the cooling sand.

They stood together as the sun disappeared and the night's first stars popped into the sky.

"I do hope you have someone," Liv said eventually. "I hate thinking of you all alone down here."

Nana took her hand. "I have everything I need."

The old fishermen gathered their chairs and shuffled off the beach. Not long after, the young couple left as well, leaning against each other, inarguably lovestruck. Only Liv and Nana remained.

A large boat slipped across the gulf in the distance, its many lights blinking in the darkness. Most of the seagulls had called it a day, but a few still soared overhead or waddled across the sand. The sound of incoming waves mesmerized Liv—she tried to imagine the vast underwater realms and all the creatures gliding through them. It was bizarre to think another world could exist right alongside you and still be just out of sight.

When an especially cool gust of wind blew in from across the water, Nana zipped her windbreaker to her chin and said maybe it was time for them to head home. Liv took one last look at the waves, slipped her shoes on, and followed Nana off the beach.

On the walk back, the neighborhood seemed like an entirely different place. Porches that had been sunny lounges only an hour ago were now shadow-filled alcoves. Grassy lawns had become featureless patches of darkness. Though a series of streetlights did their best to illuminate the area, the light they cast was ghostly and uneven. Liv linked arms with Nana and adjusted her pace until they were walking with their hips nearly brushing.

Liv spotted the church ahead on the opposite side of the street. The nativity scene sat in a poorly lit area between two streetlights. The figures were little more than lumps of gray nothingness.

Liv thought she saw one of the lumps move.

She stopped walking and squinted across the street.

"What—"

"Shh," Liv said.

The movement within the manger was subtle, a gentle swaying, and Liv wanted to believe it was only something blowing in the night breeze. But the figures and their faded clothing had all been made of solid material—ceramic statues don't blow in the wind.

Liv gulped.

The shadow seemed to turn. For a second, Liv got the impression it was looking right at her. Pinpricks of white within the darkness blinked like eyes.

Liv started to say something, to *scream* something, but then the shadow dropped out of sight. Whatever it was, it scurried around the nativity scene and skittered into the distance.

"Did you see that?" Liv asked.

"No," Nana said. "See what?"

Liv shook her head. "I don't know. Nothing, I guess. Maybe just an animal."

"You just about gave me a heart attack."

Liv said she was sorry and wrapped an arm around Nana's waist. "Let's get home."

Nana brought blankets and a pillow to the couch and told Liv she could have the bed.

"No way," Liv said. "I'm not taking your bed."

"Oh yes you are," Nana said. "I insist."

Liv shook her head vehemently. "Seriously. I wouldn't be able to sleep thinking about you twisting and turning out here."

"Because I'm such a feeble old bag of bones?"

"Exactly," Liv said. "You get it."

"Okay, fine, you win."

Liv smiled.

"Should we have a cookie and some eggnog before bed?"

"Uh, duh," Liv said.

They moved into the kitchen together and ate their snack at the table. When Liv's phone beeped, she stopped chewing and dropped her gingerbread dude to her plate. Her heart thumped, and she sucked a series of short breaths through her nose. It took her several seconds to realize a call or text couldn't be coming from anyone but her parents. Or, at worst, a wrong number. When she took the phone out of her pocket and tapped the screen, she saw a short message from her mom:

> Hope you're having a good time. Sleep tight. Love you!

Her heart slowed. She swallowed the mouthful of cookie.

Mom's texts were always so formal. Full sentences. Capital letters. Punctuation. Like she was writing a dissertation.

Liv tapped the screen and wrote back:

> i am
> nana died for a sec but i did mouth to mouth
> dont tell dad
> luv u 2!

After a second, she got a smiley emoji in response.

"What was that all about?" Nana said.

"Just Mom checking in."

Nana shook her head. "I mean why did you look so scared?"

Liv looked up at her, not wanting to lie but not wanting to get into it right now either. "I...I'll tell you later, okay?"

Nana's eyes softened. Instead of responding, she only nodded and popped the last piece of her cookie into her mouth.

When they'd finished, Liv helped Nana clean their dishes.

Then Nana said it was time to hit the sack, and Liv hugged her.

"See you in the morning. Pancakes for breakfast?"

Liv's mouth watered. "Yes!" She gave Nana another quick hug and a kiss on the cheek.

In the living room, she spread her blankets out on the couch and wrapped herself up in them. Five minutes earlier, she'd have insisted she wasn't especially tired, but as soon as her head hit the pillow, she felt sleep closing in. It was hard to believe she'd woken up in Ocala that morning. Talk about a long day.

She curled her legs, fluffed her pillow, found a comfortable position, and let herself drift away.

8

Light from the Christmas tree danced around the room, coloring the carpet, the stockings hanging from the mantel...and the two small boys sleeping on the sofa.

They lay with a head at each armrest and their legs tangled together on the middle cushion. A thin streamer of drool dangled from Evan's mouth. Kevin had no matching dangler but looked otherwise identical: dark eyebrows on a pale, round face and a little button nose above his thin mouth. If they'd both opened their eyes, you'd have seen four matching emerald irises.

They were six years old and small for their age, but the pediatrician assured their parents they were within the normal range. Height, weight, eyesight, hearing...all totally fine. Two perfectly healthy boys.

Kevin kicked out in his sleep, and Evan jerked away.

"Stop kicking," he whispered.

Kevin only snored.

Evan sighed and pulled their blanket his way a few inches.

Something whirred within the tree, an ornament with a miniature motor powering a spinning snowman. Evan opened one eye and watched the movement.

When another sound drifted in from the room down the

hall, Evan rubbed his face, opened his other eye, and propped himself up on his elbow.

"Hey," he said and shook his brother's leg.

Kevin didn't stir.

It was a sucking sound, like juice through a straw.

Evan crawled out from under the blanket. One of his colorful monster socks had twisted around his foot while he slept. When he placed his feet on the carpet, the bunched material twisted even further beneath his heel, but he didn't reach down to adjust it. As he crept across the living room, he wiped the drool from his cheek. You could see a sliver of tummy between his pajama pants and his too-small T-shirt. The blinking Christmas lights reflected off his wide, unblinking eyes.

He walked into the kitchen first, maybe expecting to find his parents or his grandfather at the refrigerator, drinking orange juice from the carton, but the kitchen was empty, silent, and dark save for the microwave's pale-green display.

When Evan stepped into the hallway leading to the bedrooms, the sucking sound intensified. He passed the bathroom—as dark and empty as the kitchen—and approached the bedroom doors so slowly that at times he didn't appear to be moving at all.

His grandpa's door was closed, and no light shone beneath it, but the other door...

He took two more short steps, peering at the gap between the door and the frame. Faint light seeped into the hall. Not an overhead light, but maybe a lamp or even someone's phone. Evan stepped into the glow.

If you'd been in the bedroom, you might have seen his tiny face slide into view. You might have seen the look of confusion that twisted into a visage of pure terror. You might have seen a dark splotch spread across the front of his pajama bottoms and trickle down his leg. And then you might have seen the large dark shape that snuck up behind him, wrapped its arms around his perfectly normal little body, and jerked him back into the darkness.

Kevin shivered and realized the blanket barely reached his waist. He pulled it to his neck and said, "Quit stealing—"

There was no second pair of legs wrapped around his own. He moved his feet back and forth and felt nothing there but the couch cushion and the blanket.

"Evan?"

He sat up and peered at the other end of the couch.

Empty.

Maybe his brother had gotten up to go to the bathroom. Maybe he could enjoy having the couch to himself for a few measly minutes.

Except he didn't hear the bathroom fan, and Evan *always* used the fan. He didn't like people to hear him potty.

Maybe Grandpa doesn't have a fan in his bathroom.

He did though. Kevin had used it himself, and he remembered it clearly because it made a scary rattling sound when he first turned it on.

If Evan was in the bathroom, he'd know.

He sat up, leaned against the sofa's armrest, and rubbed the sleep from his eyes.

"Evan?" A whisper. He didn't want to wake up his parents or his grandpa.

He peered over the side of the couch and then into the shadows on the other side of the room. He wondered if his brother might be trying to scare him.

It wouldn't be the first time.

Evan liked hiding behind doors, or in the closet, or under the bed. He loved jumping out when Kevin got near and screaming. And when Kevin screamed back (for real), Evan would laugh and laugh. Oh how he laughed. Kevin didn't know what was so funny about being a stupid little jerk.

He didn't think Evan was waiting anywhere in here though. The Christmas tree lights weren't super bright, but they lit up most of the room well enough. Kevin didn't see anywhere a person could hide.

He swung his legs over the edge of the couch and pushed the blanket off his lap.

"Evan!" Another whisper, but angrier this time.

No answer.

He padded across the living room, watching the Christmas tree, half-expecting Evan to jump out from behind it despite the clearly empty space there. Grandpa's spinning snowman buzzed, facing Kevin for a second before turning away. Back and away again. A never-ending dance.

Though he'd already decided Evan couldn't be in the bathroom, he started there anyway. The door stood open, and the bathroom was dark. Or almost. A nightlight plugged in near the sink cast a bluish glimmer across the toilet and the empty bathtub. No Evan.

He continued down the hall.

His parents had taken Grandpa's spare room. Kevin thought it looked more like an office than a bedroom, but it had a couch that folded out into a bed. They called it a *fruiton*, but Kevin thought they should have called it a foldy-bed.

"Mommy?" he said. "Daddy? Is Evan..."

He stopped. He'd reached the open door. He'd seen what lay on the fruiton.

A desk lamp cast a ray of sickly light across the room, brighter on one side and darker on the other. On the bed, two curled husks lay where his mommy and daddy should have been. That summer, he and Evan had found a dead cat behind the shed. And not recently dead either—it had been there a *long* time. You could tell because it was so shriveled, so drained of life. It had reminded them of a mummy in a scary movie their parents didn't know they'd watched. The shapes on the bed looked like the cat. Sunken. Wrinkled. Dried out. But there were two important differences: these lifeless shucks were dressed in his parents' pajamas...and they weren't alone.

Two creatures stood on either side of the bed. Their arms and legs were long and thin, spidery, but covered in skin not very unlike his own. They were naked, and one had boy parts, also long and thin. The rest of their bodies were mostly unrecognizable—lumps of jiggly flesh with zagging purple streaks that reminded him of the stretch marks on his mommy's tummy and dark, throbbing veins visible beneath their pale skin. Their necks were stumpy, almost not there at all. Piles of discarded clothing lay on the floor between their feet. When they moved, they made the sloshing sound of water balloons ready to be thrown. They bent toward the bed, dripping something red and shiny from their mouths. Their droopy, wrinkly faces could have been human, but their eyes were too big and shifted back toward their ears.

The skin dangled and swayed when they moved. They looked like creatures wearing people masks. Like Halloween backward.

If they noticed Kevin, they didn't pay him any special attention. The girl-creature lowered its mouth to the shape in his daddy's jammies and sucked. Its body jerked with every drink it took, and the punctured balloon that had been his daddy deflated. The boy-creature fed on his mommy—after each gulp, it licked the loose skin around its mouth with a lengthy black tongue.

The room stank of blood and poop and a combination of other stenches unlike anything he'd ever smelled.

He felt a scream trapped somewhere deep inside himself. It flapped around his throat, wanting to fly out but unable to find his mouth.

Then he saw the third creature. If he'd stepped farther into the room, he'd have noticed it sooner, but it stood in the corner, mostly hidden from his view behind the door. It wasn't until its own sucking sounds deepened, drowning out the others, that Kevin leaned around the door to see what was making the new, nightmarish noise.

It wasn't real. Kevin knew he must be imagining it, dreaming some terrible future in which he didn't run away and one of the creatures snatched him up and fed on him like it had fed on his parents.

He imagined the creature flicking out its inhuman tongue and slurping the blood from his pale, dead face.

Only, of course, he wasn't imagining it, and the creature wasn't holding *him*.

The monster ripped one of his twin brother's arms from his body like a turkey leg. Strips of muscle dangled from the ragged hole where Evan's arm had been, dripping blood across the carpet.

Kevin shook his head.

Not his brother. It couldn't be. His brain wouldn't accept the information as fact. In their few years of life, they'd never spent more than half a day apart. They ate together, slept together, bathed together, played together. They some-times conveyed messages to each other without ever opening their mouths. Not with mind powers or anything dumb like that, but simply with a look. That was all it took because they *knew* each other. They practically *were* each other. The idea that Kevin might have to spend even one day without his brother was unthinkable.

The creature shifted. It had a narrow face and black-marker eyes. It watched Kevin while it gnawed the arm, lick-ing gore from its wobbling mouth and cradling the remain-der of Evan's shrunken body to its chest.

Kevin's scream finally found the hole in his face and flew into the room. The creatures near the bed looked up, and the third dropped his brother's body, which hit the sodden floor with a wet thud.

The monsters converged on Kevin, scampering on their too-long legs.

He wanted to run. He wanted to scream again. But in the end, he only stood there and wondered if they'd killed his grandpa too.

His last real thought as they jerked him into the room was that it had been silly to think he'd have to spend any time alone. His time was up.

But there was one last thing he and Evan could do together...

The monsters lowered their sagging faces and tore into him. For the last few seconds of his life, Kevin watched them lap up the blood spurting from his flailing body.

9

Strawberry syrup oozed across Liv's pancakes, and she grinned.

"You're spoiling me," she said. "Seriously, how am I supposed to go back to Pop-Tarts and burnt toast after this?"

"You could always make pancakes for yourself, you know."

"Yeah right," Liv said. "Who do you think is burning the toast?"

"In that case," Nana said, "maybe stay away from my kitchen."

Melted butter swirled within her syrup. Liv licked her lips and took a bite almost too large to chew.

"Small bites," Nana said. "I thought your parents were kidding when they made me promise not to let you choke to death."

Liv swallowed her food and moaned ecstatically. The pancakes were genuinely the tastiest thing she'd eaten in as long as she could remember. Sweet and rich and unbelievably fluffy. She didn't know how a person could turn batter and heat into perfect discs of heaven, but by god, Nana had done it.

Nana sat across from her. She'd made herself two flapjacks

to Liv's three and covered them with only half as much syrup.

Two mugs of steaming coffee sat between them.

"So what's the plan for today?" Liv asked between bites.

"Whatever you want. There's a little movie theater in the community center. All the popcorn you can eat. Or we could play pool there if you feel like getting your butt kicked." She sipped from her mug.

Liv pointed her dripping fork at her. "I like your confidence."

"Or we can walk up the beach and look for seashells," Nana said, "although you usually have more luck with that earlier in the morning."

Liv swallowed another delectable bite. "What would you be doing if I wasn't here?"

Nana put a hand to her mouth, swallowed her own food, and said, "Tuesdays are usually bridge day."

"Like over troubled water?" She made an arcing motion with her hand.

Nana laughed. "No, like diamonds and hearts. A few of us get together, play a few hands, and gossip. But I let them know I had special company this week."

Liv drank her coffee. It was strong and delicious. She'd been stealing sips of her dad's coffee since she was a kid, but she'd only recently learned to really appreciate it.

"You don't have to cancel because of me," she said. "I could go with you."

"Oh, no," Nana said. "That wouldn't be any fun for you. We're just a bunch of crazy old fogies."

"I'm an old fogy at heart," Liv said, "and I'd love to meet your friends. Unless I would be like...crashing the party or whatever."

Nana waved this away. "Of course not." She took another sip. "You really want to go?"

She really did. Life down here intrigued her, and she didn't have an urge to do anything else in particular. She thought it might be easier to go back home after Christmas if she could imagine Nana down here laughing with friends instead of wandering around alone in a tearful stupor.

She said only, "Yep. Although I have no idea what bridge is. I assume something like strip poker."

Nana wrapped her hands around her mug and said, "Believe me, child, that's not something you'd want to see."

Liv shoved another potentially fatal forkful of pancakes into her mouth.

"Okay," Nana said, "let me make a call."

Harriet Ikeda met them at her front door dressed in a silky floral blouse and holding a plastic watering can.

"Good morning," Connie said and gave her a hug. Connie wasn't an especially tall woman—five three in her shoes—but the top of Harriet's head barely reached her nose. Her glasses magnified her almond-shaped, chocolate-colored eyes, and her pixie cut, still naturally dark, swished when she moved. Connie envied her the hair, though she would never admit it—she'd started to gray in her thirties and had wasted plenty of time and money on dye jobs before embracing what Henry called her *natural beauty*.

"This must be your granddaughter," Harriet said and offered her hand to Liv.

Next to Harriet, Liv was a giant. She took the small woman's hand, shook it gently, and introduced herself.

"Nice to finally meet you," Harriet said. "Your grandma never stops talking about you."

"I'm sorry."

Harriet smiled and gestured them in.

Connie had visited her neighbor hundreds of times, but she rarely left without noticing some new decoration or knickknack. The place wasn't cluttered exactly, but it was *full*. Every square inch exuded personality. Family portraits hung between framed prints and paintings. Family heirlooms and souvenirs from a lifetime of vacations sat on virtually every horizontal surface—snow globes, little statues, geodes, postcards. A minimalist Harriet was not, but things weren't tossed around the place randomly. Each item had its own special spot and a story to go with it. Harriet had shared some of those stories, but Connie knew it would take more time than either of them had left to tell them all.

Today, she spotted a new photo hanging on the hallway wall leading from the kitchen to the living room. The sepia-toned image showed a young couple posing near a cherry blossom tree. Mt. Fuji towered in the distance.

"This is new."

Harriet set the watering can down on the kitchen counter and joined her in the hallway. "I found it in an old album. My grandparents on one of their early anniversaries. Before my mom was born. Isn't it beautiful?"

Connie wasn't sure if she meant the mountain, the tree, the whole photo, or just life in general. Maybe all of the above. Regardless, it *was* beautiful, and she nodded.

Liv stood behind them, admiring the photo over their shoulders. "You look just like your grandma," she said.

It was true. Though Harriet was now much older than her grandmother had been in the photo, the resemblance was remarkable.

"And my mother too," Harriet said. "Triplets separated by time. That's what we always said." She turned away from the photo and led them to the living room.

The card table sat in its usual spot in the middle of the room, surrounded by wooden folding chairs. Ever the hospitable host, Harriet had placed an extra chair beside Connie's.

"I'm glad you could join us," Harriet said to Liv. "I was just getting ready to start some coffee. Do you drink coffee?"

Liv told her she practically bathed in it, which made Harriet chuckle. Connie appreciated her granddaughter's ability to instantly ingratiate herself with strangers. So much like her father. She wouldn't claim *full* responsibility for passing down that particular personality trait, but she also wouldn't argue if you said she deserved at least partial credit.

Connie helped ready the table while they waited for their friends. She'd phoned Herb and Pearl after talking to Harriet, and though she'd half-expected at least one of them to say they couldn't make it, that they'd made other plans, that they'd have to try again next week, they'd both sounded happy to hear the weekly game was back on. Relieved almost.

Maybe we're all too set in our ways, she thought, *unable to adapt, even to something as small as a schedule change.* It was probably true, but she didn't care. When you'd made it this far in life, you'd earned the right to be a little predictable. And never mind what anyone else might have to say about it.

Herb and Pearl arrived a few minutes later (together, Connie couldn't help but notice), and they all congregated in the kitchen, introducing themselves, questioning Liv about the drive down, life up north, school, etc., etc. When they finally moved the party to the card table, Connie couldn't help but smile. Living out her golden years in a place like this, surrounded by friends and family and happiness...it was almost perfect.

Liv thought Herb and Pearl had something going on. They weren't being obvious about it—it wasn't as if they were making out on the couch or anything—but they traded frequent glances, and Liv thought she saw more than just friendship in those looks. She *knew* she did. She wouldn't come right out and ask—she wasn't sure how things worked here, if people had secret relationships or dated around or cheated on their partners...if things were like high school, in other words —but she reminded herself to ask Nana about it later.

They gave her a crash course in bridge, and though she didn't fully understand all the intricacies, she thought she got the gist of it. And that was enough. She wasn't actually participating per se—they'd said she could play on Nana's team, but she soon realized that *play*, in her case, really meant *watch*.

Not that she minded. She was perfectly happy sitting back and watching Nana interact with her friends. They seemed like a fun gang, and she hoped she'd have a similar group of companions when she got older.

They drank coffee and tea and ate scones while they played. Liv's eyes rolled into the back of her head when she chewed the first bite of her pastry, which was full of mixed berries and covered with a thick glaze. She told herself she ought to eat something other than sugary treats at least once while she was down here, and then she told herself to shut it.

"So what are your plans for college?" Pearl said and laid down a card. She had a high-pitched, singsongy voice that reminded Liv of a cartoon character. "If you're planning on college at all, that is. My daughter tells me it's not a given these days."

Liv wiped crumbs from her lips. "I'd like to go," she said. "But I haven't narrowed down my list of options yet."

The truth was, she hadn't even *started* a list. College would be a major step, and she hadn't fully wrapped her head around the idea of it, though she definitely did want to go, and her grades and test scores were good enough to guarantee her a spot *somewhere*.

"Well, there's still plenty of time," Pearl said.

There really wasn't that much time, and Liv knew she needed to be more proactive about it.

All the school talk was giving her an unpleasant feeling in her stomach, and she decided to divert the conversation before they drove her to a full-on panic attack.

"So, how long have you all been friends?"

This, it turned out, was something they were happy to talk about. At length. Liv almost wished she hadn't asked.

Fifteen minutes later, after tales of old friendship and Herb's lost wife—gone five years now, may she rest in peace—Pearl recounted the story of rescuing Nana from an awkward conversation with a woman at the community center.

Sadie, her name was, but the way Pearl said it, it might as well have been Satan.

Liv popped the last bit of scone into her mouth and washed it down with a mouthful of coffee. They continued playing and talking. Cards flopped down on the table, and though Liv didn't entirely understand why, Pearl and Herb won the hand.

It's called a trick.

Yes, she remembered, although no one had explained *why* they called it that.

"And I thought slapjack was complicated," Liv said.

"You'll get the hang of it," Harriet said and patted her hand.

"That's what they told me about rollerblading," Liv said. "But one dead squirrel and sixteen stitches later..."

They laughed, and then Herb circled back to Pearl's story. "Speaking of Sadie, did you hear what happened?"

Nana and Harriet shook their heads. Pearl said nothing, though Liv got the impression she already knew all about it.

Herb looked at Liv, as if suddenly afraid this might not be a conversation for children. Liv didn't think of herself as a child, of course, but to the rest of them, she knew she probably looked barely out of diapers.

"It's okay," Nana said, "Liv's a tough cookie. What happened? Did she..." She cut a thumb across her throat, which elicited a hiccup of a laugh from Pearl and a disapproving glance from Harriet.

Herb shook his head. "No, but her son might have."

"*What?*"

Herb nodded and played a card. "Technically, I guess he's missing, but they found blood at the scene, and Miles Walker told me he heard the cops suspect foul play."

"That's terrible," Harriet said, although apparently it wasn't terrible enough to keep her from playing her own card.

"I guess they found a..." He looked at Liv again before continuing. "...a pool of blood in her side yard. That's the gossip anyway."

Nana shook her head. "Lord knows I'm no fan of Sadie Carter, but I wouldn't wish that on anyone."

A sense of solemnity filled the room, and they stared silently at their cards. Then Liv bumped the table's leg and apologized when everything on top took a hop to one side.

"Why would anyone want to kill Sadie's son?" Harriet said.

Herb pointed at her. "That's what I'd like to know. Not to get all spooky or anything, but if someone did kill him, there's a murderer on the loose out there."

Liv wiggled her fingers and said in her very best campfire-ghost-story voice, "Maybe in this very room."

All four heads rounded on her. Eight shocked eyes.

She stopped moving her fingers and held her hands up. "Sorry. Bad joke."

Nana shook her head. "Let's not talk about this anymore."

They agreed and returned to their game.

Liv pinched the last few crumbs of scone off her plate and poked them between her lips. "Is there a lot of crime down here?"

They all shook their heads now, but it was Herb who answered. "None. Or almost none." He played a card, the ace of spades, which must have been a good one because Harriet and Nana both harrumphed. "At least here in our dusty section of town. There are your usual arguments, and maybe even a few half-hearted fistfights, but it's quiet for the most part. Peaceful."

"It should be," Pearl said. "You don't move to God's waiting room for the action and suspense."

Harriet groaned. "I hate that phrase."

Nana said, "How do you think of it?"

Harriet waved the question away. "Never mind."

"No," Pearl said. "Come on. Tell us."

Harriet studied them for a moment before saying, "I've always thought life was like a long fall, and this place is the net that helps you land with a gentle bounce instead of a juicy splat."

Silence.

"Well hell," Herb finally said, "I don't know if that's poetic or depressing." He looked at Liv. "Pardon my French."

"Is that some kind of ancient Oriental wisdom?" Pearl said.

Nana slapped her arm gently.

"Sorry. Ancient *Japanese* wisdom?"

"Nope," Harriet said. "It's ancient circus wisdom."

Liv had been slouching. Now she sat straight up. "You were in the circus?"

Harriet smiled. "For a time."

"What was it like?"

As Harriet told her of her days under the big top, Liv found herself forgetting about everything but the small woman's soft, magical words.

This place was getting more and more exciting every second.

It was almost noon when they finally called it quits.

Herb and Pearl left first, walking beside each other up the sidewalk.

After giving Harriet another hug and thanking her for a lovely time, Nana led Liv down the porch steps.

"It was nice to meet you," Liv said over her shoulder.

"You too, dear."

They crossed Harriet's lawn, and Liv heard her door snick shut.

When they walked onto Nana's property, Liv spotted a couple pulling a pair of young kids from an old sedan parked in front of the house next door. She tried to remember the other neighbor's name, but she didn't think Nana had ever mentioned it. She'd only called her a busybody.

And there she was, the busybody herself, a slim woman with a thick hand-knit sweater and a bob of perfectly curled hair that reminded Liv of a shower cap. She stood at the top of her porch steps, arms crossed, frowning.

Nana ignored her, but Liv gave her a neighborly wave.

Busybody saw her—Liv knew she did—but she didn't return the gesture. Or acknowledge her at all. She only stood there on her porch and waited for the couple to shepherd their youngsters her way.

The little girl couldn't have been more than three or four years old. She held a stuffed monkey in one hand and sucked fiercely on the thumb of the other as she wobbled up the walkway. The little boy, a black-haired beanpole in a superhero T-shirt, ran up the porch steps and wrapped his gangly arms around Busybody's waist. She lowered a gnarled hand to his back and patted it once with what looked like slightly more affection than you'd get from bumping into a department store mannequin.

The girl saw Liv and took her thumb out of her mouth long enough to wiggle her hand in Liv's direction.

"Hi!" Liv said.

"Hewwo," the little girl said and popped her thumb back between her lips.

Busybody motioned the girl onto the porch and gave Liv a dirty look, as if she'd caught Liv trying to lure the girl into the back of a van with a handful of gummy bears.

Liv wouldn't play her game. Instead of returning the nasty look, she only smiled again and followed Nana back into her house.

After they stepped inside, her phone buzzed. She stopped, reached a shaky hand into her pocket, and held her breath as she looked at the screen.

An image came through first: Mom and Dad at the resort pool, dressed in their swimsuits and squinting into the sun, their wet hair plastered against their heads. Behind them, the pool teemed with smiling vacationers. The message that followed read:

You two should come swimming later.
The water's great!

Liv let out her breath and turned off the screen without answering. When she looked up, she saw Nana staring at her and looking concerned.

She knows something's wrong, and if you don't tell someone soon, you're gonna get some kind of stomach ulcer.

She said, "Can I talk to you about something?"

Nana told her she could talk to her about anything, scooted a chair out from under the kitchen table, and motioned for her to sit down.

Liv did. And then she gave herself permission to unburden her soul.

Connie sat across from her granddaughter, watching the girl's face twist while she tried to find the right way to start.

"I did something bad," she said finally.

Connie said nothing.

"I mean, I didn't kill anybody or anything. But...it kind of feels that way."

"Tell me." She folded her hands on the tabletop.

Liv bit her lip and looked toward the window over the sink. "It isn't even that I did something I shouldn't have," she said. "It's something I should have done and didn't."

Connie waited for clarification. She hated the worry in Liv's face. The guilt.

"Have you ever done something and had no idea why?"

"Of course." Connie nodded. "We all do things we don't fully understand sometimes. Some people spend their whole lives trying to figure out why they've done the things they've done."

"That's what I'm afraid of."

Connie realized maybe she was being less helpful than she'd intended. She tried again: "But talking can help. That's one of those old clichés that just happens to be true."

"I know," Liv said. She looked at her for just a moment before turning her attention back to the other side of the room. "I've been going over and over it in my head, but every time I feel like I might be able to forgive myself, I think about it from some new point of view and hate myself even more."

Connie reached across the table and touched Liv's hand. The girl's fingers trembled. Connie wanted to tell her not to hate herself, that she was a wonderful person, that whatever she'd done couldn't be as bad as whatever she'd built up in her mind, but she knew it would be better to let her come at it in her own way.

"I have a friend," she said. "Or *had* a friend."

Connie squeezed her hand and gave it what she hoped was a comforting pat before sliding her own hand back to her side of the table.

"Andi. Do you remember her?"

Connie said she did. Of course she did. Liv and Andi had been friends since they were small girls, since Andi's family moved to town—first or second grade maybe?—way before Connie moved down here to start what she thought of as her final life.

She remembered two little girls pushing each other on park swings, building a fort out of a refrigerator box, getting into a makeup drawer and turning each other into Frankensteinian monsters, and playing video games on the living room rug. And there were so many other things, of course. Things she'd forgotten or never known about in the first place. Things only the two girls knew. Secrets, those old airtight seals that give a friendship the buoyancy it needs to sail the seas of time.

"A few months ago," Liv said, "she told me she was...you know...into girls."

Connie nodded and continued to wait.

"And I'm totally cool with that."

"Of course," Connie said. If there was one thing her granddaughter wasn't, it was bigoted. That was another trait she hoped she could claim at least partial responsibility for passing down.

"But she hadn't told anyone else, and a few weeks ago, something happened."

Connie made a face, telling her to go on without saying a word.

Another pause.

"There's this girl," Liv said and rubbed the bridge of her nose. "Pretty. Blond. Perfect. You know the type?"

Connie said, "I've run across one or two over the years."

"This one's named Jillian. There's no, like, official ranking or anything, but if she isn't the most popular girl in school, she's up there."

Yes, Connie definitely knew the type. As a matter of fact, she'd run across more than just one or two such creatures. If she thought it might be relevant to the story, she'd have told Liv the world is full of pretty, blond, popular girls—especially if you aren't all those things yourself—but she doubted that was what Liv needed to hear at the moment. Instead, she only listened while her granddaughter continued.

"So one day after lunch, Andi found this note in her locker. From Jillian." She leaned back in her chair, eyes cutting up and to her left as she fell into her story. "It said she'd been noticing Andi noticing her. And Andi definitely had been. She told me that too. I think *dream girl* were the actual words she used."

Connie shifted slightly on her chair. It had been ages since she'd experienced what she considered a truly comfortable position, but if she kept herself moving, she could sometimes at least dull the screaming in her sorry old legs.

"There's this room in the school," Liv said. "I think maybe it used to be a janitor's closet or something, but nobody uses it for anything anymore. Well, anything except storing old junk and...you know..."

"Making out?"

Liv wrinkled her nose. As if hearing the words out loud—and from her own grandma no less—dialed up the ick factor. But she said, "Yeah. And probably more than that."

Connie gave her a look.

Liv held up a hand. "Not that I know anything about that. Just rumors."

"Okay."

"Anyway, the note said Jillian wanted to meet Andi there after school so they could *explore*. That's what she said. Explore."

"Enticing."

"Exactly," Liv said. "I can't imagine what must have been going through Andi's head. Probably a little bit of everything."

Connie thought Liv was likely right about that.

"And I think part of me knew something was wrong even then," Liv said. "I mean, it was nothing I could put my finger on, but it just seemed..."

"Too good to be true?"

"Yes! That's it."

"But you didn't want to rain on her parade?"

Liv nodded and blew a loose strand of hair off her face. "I thought if she knew I had doubts, she'd think it was because I didn't think she was...worthy or whatever."

Connie thought high school must be a total minefield for these poor kids. It had been hard enough in her day. "So what happened?"

Liv stuck her thumbnail between her teeth and nibbled it for a second before realizing what she was doing and jerking her hand away from her mouth. She'd had a terrible nail-biting habit when she was younger and had worked hard to quit —Connie had a sudden, clear memory of a very young Liv crying over her bloody little fingers.

"In PE later," Liv said, "I overheard Jillian and her friends laughing about something. They were whispering, and maybe they thought I couldn't hear, but I think they probably didn't even realize I was there. Or maybe forgot who I was."

Connie shifted again.

"They were planning something. I couldn't hear it all, and they weren't exactly laying it all out like bad-movie villains, but I heard enough to know they were planning on recording something."

Connie thought she saw where this was going.

"I confronted them and asked what they were talking about, but they pushed me down and told me to mind my own business."

Connie sucked air through her teeth. "Those little bitches."

This brought a real smile to Liv's face, but it dropped away quickly. "I keep trying to tell myself that I didn't know for sure they were planning on messing with Andi, and I guess technically that's true, but it's also just an excuse, you know?"

Connie did.

"But the thing is, what if they *had* been talking about something else? What if Jillian really did want to *explore* with Andi and I said something and ruined it? That's what I told myself anyway. Even though I knew it was probably bull."

"I take it they *were* talking about Andi?"

Liv nodded. "And it gets worse."

"I figured it might."

"So Jillian met Andi in the...make-out room after school, but she'd set up her phone somewhere. Somewhere hidden I guess. I'm still not sure about that part. But anyway, they did some, you know, kissing and stuff, and then..." Liv blew out a long breath. "She convinced Andi to take off her shirt and bra."

"Oh no."

"And then, before anything else could happen, she grabbed her clothes and ran away with them."

"Jesus."

"And when Andi ran out after her, Jillian's friends were all standing there with their phones out."

Connie closed her eyes. *That poor, poor girl.*

"She's super self-conscious about her body," Liv said. "I don't really know why. I mean, I guess we all are, right? But it's especially bad for her."

Connie remembered Andi as a beautiful young lady, but she knew other people's opinions or even undeniable objective reality didn't matter much when it came to someone's self-image. She knew perfectly well how hard it could be to appreciate yourself when the world was intent on showing you only the most beautiful flukes of nature.

"She covered herself the best she could," Liv continued, "but you can only cover so much. And they just kept filming." The last word came out with a hiss that made Connie shudder.

Liv took a deep breath. "She ran away, and someone gave her a hoodie or something eventually, but not before they had all the footage they needed."

Connie wiped a tear from her cheek.

"Jillian edited everything together and uploaded the video."

"No," Connie said. "She didn't, did she?"

Liv wiped away her own tear. "Everyone in school had seen it by the next day. And..." Now the tears came pouring down Liv's face. "Someone sent it to her parents. That's...how they found out about...you know."

Connie grabbed Liv's hand again. The girl's whole body hitched.

"That Jillian girl is beyond sickening," Connie said, "but I don't understand why you're blaming yourself for any of this."

"Because..." She wiped her nose with the back of her hand. "Jillian or one of her friends told Andi I knew. That I knew and did nothing. And when Andi asked me, what could I say? I *did* know, and I *didn't* say anything, and I don't even really know *why*." She buried her face in her hands and bawled.

Connie scooted her chair around the table and wrapped her arm around Liv's quaking shoulders.

"Pretty soon," Liv said through her hands, "everyone at school was sending me nasty texts. Like I was the bad guy."

Connie leaned her head against Liv's and stroked her hair.

"And maybe I *am* the bad guy. I could have warned her. I could have *tried* at least." Liv moved her hands away from her face, pulled away slightly, and looked at Connie. Her eyes were red, wet, and full of confusion. "Am I the bad guy?"

"Oh, honey." Connie wrapped her arms around Liv and squeezed her as hard as she could. "Of course not."

"Then why do I feel like I am?"

Connie thought for a second before answering—she wanted to be sure she got this right. "Because you're a kind person," she said. "The kindest. You have the biggest heart I've ever seen. And you wish you could have done something to protect your friend. That's all. Have you talked to her?"

Liv shook her head. "I tried, but she...blocked me." Fresh tears dripped down her face as she told Connie about her ever-buzzing phone, the never-ending series of threats and ugly messages from her schoolmates, and the decision to leave the device home so she wouldn't have to deal with it.

"You two have been friends practically your whole lives," Connie said. "I think once you've had a chance to explain everything, she'll forgive you."

Liv didn't look convinced.

"I know it seems bad," Connie said, "and sometimes it feels like running away would be so much easier, but if you face the trouble instead, it's usually not as hard to overcome as you thought. Take it from someone who's lived a lot of life and faced plenty of trouble herself."

"Did you ever want to run away?"

Connie nodded. "Not only did I want to, I *did*."

"And what happened?"

"It ate me up inside." Connie stroked Liv's hair again.

"So you think I should talk to her?"

"Definitely," Connie said. "And in person if possible. Once she sees the sorrow in your eyes, you might not have to say a word. It's perfectly clear how much you care about her."

"I love her," Liv said. "She's like my sister." She wiped at her eyes. "No, she *is* my sister. Or the closest thing to it I'm ever going to have."

Connie gave her another squeeze and told her everything was going to be all right. Eventually, Liv's hitching body began to still. She leaned her head against Connie's shoulder and sniffled.

"Thanks," Liv said after a minute. "I obviously needed to get that out."

"Anytime." Connie kissed the side of her head. "You can always talk to me about anything."

Liv gave her a crushing hug that felt like it might pulverize her ribs. She said nothing.

"Mom texted just before we started talking," Liv said and pulled away. "She asked if we wanted to go swimming."

"Do you?" The pain in her ribs subsided, and she sucked in a deep breath.

Liv nodded. "Yeah, I think it would be nice."

"Then swimming we shall go," Connie said and gave the table a gentle slap. "Let's grab our suits."

10

Fred stood in the back yard behind a row of evergreen bushes while he waited for Agnes and Dorothea to join him. The last of the day's light had drained from the sky. Clouds and seagulls slipped across the half-full moon.

When Agnes dropped a hand on his shoulder, he didn't flinch—he'd smelled them approaching. Dorothea sidled up next to them and licked her lips.

The yard was a pool of shadows. Across it, people moved behind lit windows.

"How many?" Dorothea whispered.

"Two kids," Fred said, "and the parents. Nora's a piece of work, but nothing to worry about."

"Should we turn her?" Agnes said.

Fred shook his head vigorously. "Definitely not." *We have one too many domineering women around here as it is*, he wanted to say but didn't.

Agnes nodded her understanding. Her blue hair had gone dark. Not quite black, but a thick, lustrous brown that *looked* black in the dim moonlight. The baggy skin under her eyes had tightened and her lips had plumped. He'd kissed those lips once, and though that had been over a hundred years ago and she'd made it perfectly clear it could never happen again, he still remembered the way they tasted.

Of the three of them, Dorothea's looks had improved the most. Her neck no longer wobbled, which intensified the severity of that knife-blade visage of hers. And some of the milky quality in her eyes had cleared away, leaving only a sense of ultra-awareness. Her skin, always surprisingly clear even at the peaks of her aging cycle, looked downright flawless now.

Fred knew he also looked significantly better. His dark hair flowed across his head in thick waves, and his twisted back had gone ramrod straight. Energy coursed through his body, and his heart thumped steadily behind his less-saggy man boobs.

"Ready?" Dorothea asked them.

Agnes nodded, and after only a slight hesitation, Fred did the same.

They couldn't fully transform.

Because of you.

Yes, fine. He'd jumped the gun, and they were all paying the price for it.

But they could get close enough. Close enough to feed anyway, and that was all that really mattered at the moment. The next cycle would be more difficult, and it might take several to get things fully back on track, but they would manage.

They'd done it before.

They waded into the pool of shadows, approached the small house, and honed in on another delicious helping of youth.

When they returned from the resort, they parked Connie's car at the curb in front of her cottage. She had a designated spot in the resident lot at the end of the block, and they'd walked down to retrieve the car earlier, but neither of them felt like making the walk again, and there was no rule against leaving the car on the street for a while. Connie would return it to the lot later.

Liv hopped out of the passenger seat and waited for Connie on the sidewalk with her arms crossed over her stomach, bouncing slightly. A cold front had moved in from the northwest, a breath of genuine December air that blew through the neighborhood, tousled the girl's hair, and shook the palm fronds.

Liv grinned and brushed her hair out of her face. Her mood had improved drastically since their earlier conversation. At the pool, she'd splashed around happily with a group of young girls, throwing pool toys so they could dive in and fetch them and engaging in a screeching game of war with some colorful water guns. She hadn't mentioned her friend again, and Connie hadn't pressed her. If she wanted to talk about it, she could, and Connie would be there to listen. If not...well, that was fine too.

She locked the car and wrapped her arm around Liv's when she offered it. They approached the house together.

Inside, Liv told her she'd like to take a quick shower before dinner. They'd changed out of their swimsuits at the hotel but hadn't taken the opportunity to rinse off the chlorine. Although Connie hadn't spent as much time in the pool as Liv—had only really stuck her legs in for a bit while she talked to Benji and Em—she thought she wouldn't mind a shower herself, once Liv was done.

For now, she ground some beans and started a fresh pot of coffee. She generally tried not to drink caffeine after midday, but she had a craving, and what was life without an exception to the rules here and there? While the coffee brewed, she slipped out of her shoes and walked into her bedroom. At her dresser, she opened the lid of an antique jewelry box that had been her grandmother's, her mother's, and finally hers. She rummaged through rings, earrings, brooches, and trinkets until she found the necklace.

She pulled it out and held it up. The silver chain needed a good polish, but the translucent, sea-green pendant glittered. It was a simple teardrop necklace, just costume jewelry really, and though there wasn't anything inherently fancy about it, the fact that she still had it after all these years seemed like nothing short of a miracle.

She sat on the edge of the bed, turning the pendant over in her hands and remembering.

A minute after the shower shut off, Liv called out for her and joined her in the bedroom. She ran a brush through her damp hair as she crossed to the bed in a fresh pair of pajamas.

Connie patted the mattress beside her, and Liv plopped down.

"I want to give you something."

Liv raised her eyebrows and stopped brushing.

"When I was a girl, my best friend in the world, Alice, gave me this necklace for my birthday." The pendant had a nick on one edge, the result of a childhood bike crash that had left Connie with a broken arm and kicked off the most utterly boring summer of her life. She fingered the nick. "For many, many years, I never took it off."

"And you want to give it to me?"

Connie nodded. "You can keep it, or you can give it to your friend after you make up."

"*If* we make up."

"After," Connie said, trying to convey absolute confidence.

Liv shook her head. "I can't take that," she said. "It's too special."

Connie took Liv's hand and drizzled the necklace into her cupped palm. "*You* are special," she said, "and it was going to be yours eventually anyway."

Liv let the chain slip between her fingers and held the pendant up to the light. "It's beautiful. Thank you." She gave Connie's hand a squeeze and asked if she'd help her put it on.

Connie looped the chain around Liv's neck and fastened the clasp.

Liv held the pendant for a second before letting it fall to her shirt. "What happened to Alice?"

Connie gulped. She supposed she should have expected the question, but she hadn't, and it hit her hard. "She...died," she said. "In a car accident right before we graduated high school." She felt tears dribbling down her face.

"Oh..." Liv hugged her again. "I'm so sorry," she whispered into her ear.

"It was a long time ago," Connie said. But for just a second, she remembered it as if it had been only yesterday: the smell of the flower-filled funeral home, the sound of weeping family members and friends, the overhead lights reflecting off the glossy coffin, which they'd kept closed to spare everyone the gruesome proof of human fragility.

Liv hadn't let Connie go, but she stiffened suddenly.

"What's—"

"What is that?" Liv said.

Still lost in memories of her friend, Connie pulled back and saw a combination of confusion and fear in the girl's eyes.

"What's what?"

Liv untangled herself from Connie, hurried over to the bedroom window, and slid the sheers aside. "Quick," she said, "turn off the light."

Connie did and then joined Liv.

She looked past the row of bushes separating her yard from Nora's. Light from the neighboring windows cut across the darkness between the properties.

"I don't see—" But then she did. Something streaked past the open curtains directly across from them, a long-armed, amorphous shape that Connie could make no sense of. She removed her glasses, wiped the lenses on her blouse, and slipped them back onto her face.

Through Nora's window, she saw the corner of some piece of furniture. Maybe a dresser. She'd never been inside the house, but she guessed she might be looking into the woman's bedroom.

A hand reached up from below the window, grasped the edge of the dresser, and tensed. Connie watched her neighbor pull herself up from the floor, rising into view slowly, shakily. Streaks of blood marred her nightgown. Her right eye had swollen shut, like a boxer's, the eyeball tucked away behind a lump of puffy, purple flesh. She slapped the window with one hand and screamed. Even across the distance and through multiple panes of glass, the scream sounded unnervingly close. As if she were in the room with them, screeching in their ears.

Then something else slid into view. A thin limb that might have been a pale tree branch if not for the five clawlike fingers at the end of it. It grabbed Nora's face. The woman slapped the window one last time before the limb yanked back and jerked her out of view.

"Oh my god," Liv said. Her face pressed against the window. "Someone is attacking her." She turned away from the glass and looked at Connie, her eyes wild. "Someone is attacking Busybody!"

Connie's mind was a mess of disconnected thoughts. Who was Busybody? What was *happening*?

"Do you have a weapon?" Liv said.

"I—"

"We have to help them."

Connie shook her head and tried to get her thoughts under control. She grabbed Liv's shoulders. "We have to call the police."

"Yes," Liv said, "I know. Of course. But then we have to *help* them. There are kids over there. Little kids."

Connie only shook her head again. "I don't think we *can*," she said. "It's—"

Liv shook out of her grasp. "We have to try," she said.

Connie thought of the inhuman arm and Nora's heart-wrenching squeal.

"You call the police," Liv said. "I'm going to help. I can't do nothing."

Connie reached for her, intending to grab her, to wrap her arms around her and drag her to the ground if she had to. But she was too late—Liv had already slipped beyond her reach.

Liv ran to the kitchen, grabbed a knife from the block beside the gurgling coffee maker, and hurried back through the house, holding the blade away from her body as she ran past the dangling stockings and twinkling tree. When she slid open the patio door, cool air blew into her face. Her thin pants and sleep shirt billowed in the breeze, and she suddenly realized she was barefoot, but she didn't want to go back for her shoes. Every second could count.

She moved across the patio and into the grass, praying she wouldn't step on a sharp stick or rock, and adjusted her grip on the knife's handle.

What am I doing?

She had no idea. She was no hero. Other than a few self-defense classes she and her mom had taken a few years ago, she knew nothing about fighting. She couldn't even remember how to throw a punch (was it thumb over the fingers or under?), and although she supposed she was relatively fit, she was definitely no stronger than the average person. She didn't even know what to do with the knife, for crying out loud. Unless the people attacking Busybody were made of vegetables.

People?

That was the other thing. Liv wasn't sure what she'd seen through the neighbor's window, but it definitely hadn't been a normal human arm.

Someone in a costume?

Maybe.

An animal?

That seemed less likely, but not impossible.

Whatever it had been, the memory of it chilled her.

She pushed through the bushes separating the two back yards, scanning the area, half-expecting something to jump out at her, trying to listen for sounds over the thumping of her heart.

She remembered what Herb had said about the missing man, the police suspecting foul play, and the possibility that there might be a killer on the loose. Then she remembered the eyes she'd seen by the nativity scene when she and Nana had come home from the beach.

What am I going to find in that house?

She hustled across Busybody's yard and approached the back deck in a kind of crouch, tiptoeing through the grass.

The back door was open. Just a crack. A pair of wooden steps led up to the deck. Liv placed a bare foot on the first, listened for movement inside the house, and climbed another step. A glowing window looked out on the deck. She ducked and crept beneath it, praying no one would glance out and see the top of her bobbing head.

She continued across the deck, expecting the boards to creak beneath her feet, looking for the best potential escape route if something came rushing at her. Wind blew her damp hair across her face, giving her a false sense of constant movement and pushing her to the brink of a panic attack.

When someone in the house screamed, she told herself to run away, to do the smart thing even if it felt wrong. Her disobedient feet carried her toward the door instead. She pushed it open, glaring at her traitorous hand but unable to stop herself from slipping through the doorway.

Hyperventilating, squeezing the handle of the knife so tightly her fingers throbbed, she walked into a small kitchen.

The lights were on, but the room was empty. A vintage re-frigerator dominated the opposite wall, towering over a scarred wooden table that filled most of the floor space be-tween the cabinets. Liv circled the table, watching the door-way across the room and trying to control her erratic breathing.

Another scream. A child's terrified wail. And beyond that, the gentle tones of Christmas music playing somewhere deeper within the house.

Liv hurried to the doorway and peeked around the frame.

In the living room, a creature hovered over the little girl Liv had seen earlier that day. She'd seemed terribly young before, sucking her thumb and trailing her brother up the walkway, but now she looked younger still, not much older than a toddler. Tears poured down her face and across her fluttering lips. Her stuffed monkey lay on the floor nearby, just out of her reach.

The creature was unlike anything Liv had ever seen. If she melded every monster from every scary movie she'd ever watched with the terrors from her worst nightmares, the combination might have resembled the first step in some nasty transformation that led ultimately to this aberration. The beast's limbs were gangly to the point of structural insta-bility. Its lump of a torso had a cancerous-looking bulge at the upper end that must have been the back of its head, and its wrinkly, veiny flesh seemed putrefied. Liv couldn't see its face from her position, and she knew without question that she didn't *want* to see it, that if the monster turned and looked at her, she'd faint. Or even die. Anyone who said you couldn't die of fright had never seen *this*.

Although the creature didn't seem aware of Liv's presence

yet, the girl spotted her between the thing's elongated legs. Her eyes widened, and she reached forward with one chubby-fingered hand.

Hewwo.

The earlier greeting floated through Liv's mind, but she knew the gesture meant something different this time. Not *Hello* but *Help me!*

Not aware she was going to do it, Liv bared her teeth and ran at the monster's back, raising the knife over her head, ready to plunge it into whatever bit of vulnerable flesh she could find.

When she was only one giant step away and starting to think she might reach the creature unnoticed, it spun toward her, arcing one of those broomstick arms around in a vicious swipe that knocked her off her feet and into the artificial Christmas tree on the other side of the room.

Liv hit the tree with a crunch of shattering ornaments. Her spine struck the trunk, knocking the tree over, and her breath exploded out of her body like air from a popped tire. Tree limbs scraped across her arms and face. Bunches of vinyl needles probed her ears, nose, and mouth. She dropped into a pile of gifts, felt their corners against her neck and between her ribs. One gift bag skittered across the floor, toppled over, and birthed a cotton dolly with a wide, toothless grin.

Now she saw the monster's face, a wedged nightmare of a thing, and she'd been right to fear the sight of it. Its eyes were enormous and emotionless, positioned toward the back of its head like a bug's. Its skin hung from the underlying structure like melted cheese and jiggled when it moved. The lips surrounding its oversized mouth were thick and cracked, and bloody saliva dripped from its multiple rows of sharklike teeth.

The creature screeched at the doll and then at Liv. The sound reminded her of feedback from the school auditorium's loudspeakers. She wanted to slap her hands against her ears to block the head-splitting howl, but she couldn't seem to move her arms.

I'm paralyzed. My spine hit the tree and snapped, and now—

But no, she wasn't paralyzed, only stunned. She could feel her feet and wiggle her fingers.

Her empty fingers.

She'd lost the knife.

The creature looked down at the squirming girl, then it picked her up and held her above its head.

"Leave her alone!" Liv screamed at the thing in a gravelly, broken voice. She tried to sit, pressing down on one of the gifts for leverage, and pushed herself up. The box crumpled beneath her weight, whatever had been inside it crackled like broken glass, and she fell back to her side. She tried again, found the floor between the boxes and pushed against that. This time, she managed to get into a sitting position. Somewhere a million miles away, the Christmas music continued.

The monster licked its lips with a dark, over-long tongue and brought the girl closer to its mouth.

"No!"

It looked from the girl to Liv—back and forth several times, slowly—before finally pulling its arm back like a pitcher throwing a fastball and hurling the child across the room.

The little girl spun through the air, her hair swirling around her head and hiding her screeching mouth. She flew through an archway between the living room and the adjoining hall and hit the hallway wall with a meaty thump and a crack of drywall. The sound she made when she dropped to the floor was even louder, like the thud of a stomping foot.

The girl's crying stopped instantly.

She didn't move.

Liv wanted to run to her, but she once again found herself unable to control her body. She only sat there beneath the ruined tree, gasping, while a second creature slunk into view, plucked the girl off the floor, and carried her out of sight.

Liv faced the first creature again. Her facial muscles twitched, and though she wanted to cry, she felt herself harden instead. "You bastard," she said.

The creature grinned, and it was the most terrifying thing Liv had ever seen. Those rows and rows of teeth seemed to go on forever, like some kind of optical illusion.

It took a step toward her, moving with an awful sloshing sound. Its feet were wide, flipper-like slabs of gnarled meat, and they slapped the floor when it moved. Liv swept her hands through the crushed Christmas presents, looking for the knife but finding only ribbon and scraps of torn wrapping paper.

As the creature moved closer, it reached toward her with its clawed hands. Blood vessels throbbed beneath its skin. Its eyes gleamed within its wobbling mask of a face.

Liv smelled it now, a mingled stench of blood and sweat, the nauseating funk of rotten food. Every cell in her body told her to get up, to run, but she had nowhere to go. The creature had cornered her, literally, and with its inhuman reach, there was no way to maneuver around it.

She did the only thing she could think to do: she picked

up one of the presents beside her leg and brandished it like a weapon, ready to swing it at the monster's head or maybe throw it in its face to distract it. Something. The fact that the gift weighed almost nothing, that it most likely contained an article of feather-light clothing, was something Liv decided she'd just have to ignore.

Her body trembled. She opened her mouth to scream, but then a peal of thunder *boomed* through the room, and the creature's face exploded.

Blood and bits of pulverized organic matter sprayed across the room, showering the floor, the toppled tree, the pile of half-crushed Christmas presents...and Liv. The gore hit her face and open mouth, hot and thick.

She heard nothing but an uninterrupted ringing and a dull *whump* that might have been her heart.

Where the monster's face had been, there was now only a dripping crater. Brains, shards of shattered teeth, and a single eyeball with a tail of nerves and sinew dribbled from the ragged opening. Then the thing dropped forward, flopping against the floor only inches from Liv with a muffled thump that sounded impossibly distant.

Nana stood where the creature had been, holding a smoking revolver in both hands, her eyes cartoonishly wide behind the magnifying lenses of her glasses.

Liv stared at her for a second, stunned, and then leaned to the side and vomited.

"What...is that?" Nana said. The words were deadened and nearly indecipherable.

Liv shook her head, wiped puke and blood from her lips, and said, "I don't know, but it isn't alone." Her own words sounded muffled as well, but the ringing had faded slightly.

She pointed at the archway, to the spot where the second creature had grabbed the girl.

Nana raised the gun and pointed it in that direction. "Let's get out of here. Get up and stay behind me," she said.

Liv shook her head again. "The kids. They might not be... we might still be able to help them."

On the floor, the creature's body moved. Nana spun back toward it, angling the gun down, and shot it again, in the center of its grotesque torso this time. The recoil kicked her arms up, and Liv couldn't believe she didn't drop the weapon. The body bucked, but the shot hadn't been necessary. The monster wasn't getting up. It wasn't alive. It was *morphing*.

The long arms and legs shortened and thickened as the rest of the body compressed, transforming into something almost human shaped. The metamorphosis produced a series of crunching sounds and a sudden whiff of flatulence that was nastier than anything Liv had ever smelled.

Nana kept her gun pointed at the body until it stopped twitching. They were left staring at the naked backside of a seemingly ordinary human woman.

"What in the world?" Nana said.

Liv leaned down, wondering if she should flip the body over before remembering it had no face. That *she* had no face.

No, that wasn't right. Whatever the creature was, it wasn't a normal woman, despite how it now looked. Neither a she nor an it but something in between.

Wavy, chestnut-colored hair covered the back of the creature's head, but you could still see the hole where Nana's bullet had entered its skull. The second bullet wound marked its back near the spine. Liv definitely didn't want to see what *that* exit wound might look like.

"We have to leave now," Nana said. "Liv?" Her eyes were full of confusion and terror, and Liv realized she had no idea what must be going through the woman's mind. What did it feel like to slay a monster?

Liv said, "The kids," and looked toward the hallway again.

The second creature's head protruded just beyond the doorframe, studying them with its abyssal eyes, baring those endless teeth.

Nana raised the gun and fired at it. The bullet missed by only inches, striking the hallway wall and leaving a hole the size of a softball in the drywall. Although the gun didn't seem especially large, it must have been more powerful than it looked, because it seemed like she was shooting freaking cannonballs. The creature screeched and scurried away. The sound of its loud, slapping feet made it sound less like a solitary creature and more like a stampede.

Liv hurried after it, her bare feet sliding through the blood fanned across the floor. Nana caught up to her, tugged her shoulder, and moved into the hallway just ahead of her. She fired the gun again, but Liv couldn't see her target. By the time she circled around the doorframe, the creature had disappeared into a bedroom at the end of the hall.

"Stay behind me," Nana said again and shuffled after it.

The tinkling sound of breaking glass echoed down the hallway. They reached the bedroom door just in time to see not one but two more creatures squeezing through a broken window. Though Liv caught only a glimpse of their fleeing forms, it was enough to see the object the second creature clutched in its malformed hand: Hewwo Girl, split nearly in half and dangling from the creature's fingers in mangled strips of half-chewed flesh.

Liv wanted to scream but couldn't. A sudden encompassing sorrow left her feeling emptied, unable to cry, unable to speak. The creatures' footsteps trailed off into the distance, and wind blew past the broken window. When she turned her attention back into the bedroom, she saw the monsters' leavings: a pile of bodies on the floor, straight out of some graphic war documentary. The dark-haired boy lay atop the pile—his head hung upside down over a hip that must have been his mother's. He looked like juiced fruit, sunken and colorless. His parents' bodies lay in a tangle beneath him, twisted into such broken, unnatural positions that you couldn't tell where one began and the other ended. Busybody lay at the bottom of the dogpile. One aged hand had come to rest near the perimeter of the mess, and it took Liv a second to realize it wasn't attached to anything. Its ragged stump dripped into the puddle of fluids spreading away from the corpses.

The Christmas music she'd heard earlier came from a radio on the nightstand across the room. She wanted to run to it and rip its plug from the wall, silence its inappropriate noise for good, but that would mean walking right past the pile of bodies, and she wouldn't do that.

Nana uttered a sound that might have been a gasp or a sob and squeezed Liv's shoulder. Liv flinched away instinctively before turning to her and wrapping both arms around her neck.

"We *really* have to go," Nana said.

"Okay," Liv said. "And we should call the police. I don't know what they can do against those...things, but we should still try, right?"

"I already called," Nana said. "From the house." She cocked her head, as if listening for sirens. "For now, I want to get away from here. Those things could be anywhere."

"Okay," Liv said, "but where can we go? Not your house—they could be in there. They could be...waiting for us." She didn't know if it was true, if the things—whatever they were—were capable of such tactical thinking, but she couldn't rule it out, and she wouldn't risk it.

"No," Nana agreed. "The car's still parked out front." She reached into her pocket and pulled out her keys. "We'll go back to the resort. We'll be safe there."

Liv nodded, followed Nana away from the massacre, and tried to convince herself there might be such a thing as safety anywhere in the world.

They scuttled across the yard, through an unlocked door, and into the neighbor's empty living room. Fred paused until he was sure no one had followed before offering the rest of the meat to Agnes. Then he stepped back and began to revert.

The change felt like burning alive, and though he knew the agony lasted only a few seconds, it always seemed to go on forever. He clenched his jaw, and the sensation spread through his quivering body. When the transition was complete, he stood with his hands on his knees, huffing and naked.

Energy coursed through his body. Immense strength. Staggering vitality. If he'd looked into a mirror right then, he guessed he'd appear no older than forty.

While Agnes drained the last useful fluids from the girl's withered body, Fred stood in the center of the room and combed his hands through his ever-thickening hair.

Images of Dorothea ran through his mind. Cooling in a plash of her own blood next door. Diminished, as if she'd never been anything but another worthless human, as if she hadn't been the most powerful, vicious being he'd ever known.

Gone now. Truly gone. And it was all his fault.

He'd been impatient and weak, and because of that weakness, they'd been forced to start the cycle far too early. By next Christmas, they could have transitioned fully and bullets would have bounced right off their iron-dense hides.

They'd always known they weren't immortal, of course, but after spending so many years dancing deftly out of death's path, knowing and believing had become two separate things. How could a hunk of metal the size of a fingertip end a centuries-long reign? It was ridiculous.

He crossed the room, screamed, and knocked over the Christmas tree. Ornaments clattered to the ground, and after a dying flash, the tree's lights darkened.

Behind him, Agnes shifted. When he turned to face her, he saw the last of her blood-drenched fingers shorten. The girl's depleted body lay facedown at her feet. Agnes shook gently, and though she'd regained most of her prime beauty, he barely glanced at her body.

"What is it?" she said. "Where's Thea?"

Fred crossed the room, grabbed her shoulders, and said, "I'm sorry."

"Where is she?"

Fred looked up at the ceiling, then back into Agnes's eyes. "She's dead."

Agnes pushed him away and shook her head. "No." She took a step toward the door, as if to go back and see for herself, and then stopped. "How?"

"The neighbor," he said and gestured around the room with his head. "This bitch. Connie what's her face. She shot her."

"Are you sure? Maybe—"

"I'm sure," Fred said.

Tears streamed down her face. She turned away from him and sobbed. He considered trying to comfort her but knew that was probably the last thing she wanted. Instead, he scanned the room, meaning only to give his eyes something to do while he waited for her to grieve, and spotted a newfangled phone on the end table beside the couch. He picked it up.

When she'd cried herself out (for now anyway—he had no doubt there would be more tears later), she took a shaky breath and said, "What should we do?"

"I just got an idea," he said, still looking at the phone. "We feed one last time. A real feast. Then we'll clean up the loose ends and get out of here. Somewhere far away. Somewhere we can start over fresh."

"A feast?" She turned to him, wiping her face.

"With a side of revenge."

She furrowed her brow but said nothing. He turned the phone toward her. The image on the screen showed a pool full of mouth-watering treats. On a glass door in the background, you could clearly see the words *The Beachside Resort Lounge and Bar*. The couple in the foreground and the message below left little doubt as to who'd sent the text.

"The bitch's family?" Agnes said.

Fred nodded and studied the stockings on the decorative mantel across the room: Livinia, Benjamin, Emily, and Constance. Connie...Connie something. They'd seen her around, of course, but if he'd ever known her last name, he couldn't recall it now. He searched the room for a minute, found a stack of mail, and got the name from behind one of the little plastic windows, hoping it would be enough.

"What do we do about Dorothea's...body?"

Fred shook his head. "We have to leave it. She'd understand."

"Should we get—"

"No," Fred said. "Not yet. Not if we don't have to."

In the distance, sirens warbled.

"We have to go," he said. "But first..."

He got a bottle of rubbing alcohol from the bathroom and a handful of rags and a lighter from the kitchen, moving with an agility he hadn't possessed even an hour earlier. He spritzed the rags with alcohol, placed them in a few strategic places, and then splashed the rest of the liquid around the room.

"What are you doing?"

Fred lit the rags, finishing with the one he'd placed beneath the Christmas tree, and grinned when the flames spread to the pile of surrounding gifts. "Creating a distraction," he said. "*Now* let's go."

They hurried out of the house, retrieved their clothes from beside the pile of bodies next door, and disappeared into the night.

In Connie's cottage, fire crawled across the couch cushions and up the walls. Christmas gifts crackled as their wrapping paper wrinkled and blackened. Curtains billowed when flickering flames climbed their folds.

The first stocking to catch fire was Connie's. The toe singed and then ignited—hand-stitched seams split and smoked. Less than a minute later, all four stockings had dropped from their hangers. They burned together in a pile on the floor.

When the flames crawled over the tiny body in the center of the room, its shriveled flesh sizzled.

By the time the approaching sirens arrived, the fire had become an unstoppable inferno. Thick black smoke billowed into the cooling Florida sky, and rubbernecking neighbors shuffled onto their porches and stoops to gawk at the commotion.

11

Liv sat in Nana's passenger seat, fiddling with the dashboard controls, trying to warm up the car and stop herself from shivering, though she knew the shaking probably had more to do with shock than temperature.

Nana clutched the steering wheel with both hands and stared unblinkingly at the road ahead.

I don't think I'm the only one in shock.

She wondered if Nana should be driving, if it was safe, but she wasn't sure what other option they had. She definitely didn't trust herself behind the wheel right then, and they desperately needed to get away.

What had those things been?

She had no idea. She'd never seen or even heard of anything like them. Part vampire maybe? Part werewolf? Something entirely different? Ancient, misunderstood monstrosities on which the stories of all those other creatures had been based?

Maybe. In the end, she guessed it didn't really matter. Whatever they were, they were here, and they were real, and she'd only barely escaped them. Thanks to Nana.

"You saved my life," she said.

Nana turned to her for just a second while slowing for a red light. "Of course," she said.

"Thank you."

Nana placed a wrinkled hand on Liv's knee until the light turned green. "I just wish I could have gotten there in time to save everyone." Her voice hitched on the last word. Fresh tears dribbled down her cheeks.

Liv thought of a certain stuffed monkey that would never be reunited with its pretty little girl, of the wisps of hair swirling around the girl's head while she sailed through the last few moments of her life. "We couldn't have gotten there any sooner," she said. "We did everything we could." Trying to convince herself as much as Nana.

Heat pumped from the vents, and though she hadn't stopped shaking, Liv felt sweat running down her back. She spun the controls to turn off the heater and flipped down the visor so she could look at herself in the mirror.

Streaks of blood crossed her shirt, face, and hair. She never would have imagined the most gruesome thing she'd see in her life would be her own reflection, but here she was, staring at herself and disgusted to the point of nausea.

"There are some wet wipes in the glove box," Nana said. "It won't be enough, I know, but maybe better than nothing. We'll get you cleaned up when we get to the room."

The room. Until that second, the idea of returning to the resort had been nothing but an abstract thought, but now that she'd begun to process things, she thought of her parents, who were totally clueless to the night's goings-on.

"What will we tell Mom and Dad?"

"The truth, I guess," Nana said. "Eventually. But we don't need to worry about that right now."

"Why not?" She found a stack of individually wrapped wet

wipes, tore open the first, and did her best to wipe the gore off her forehead.

Nana didn't respond for a moment. Liv finally looked over at her. "What?"

"I wasn't supposed to say anything," Nana said, "but I guess everything's different now anyway." She chewed her bottom lip and glanced in Liv's direction.

"What?"

"Your parents aren't at the hotel."

"They aren't?" She stopped wiping her face and dropped her hands to her lap. "Where are they?"

"At dinner with a real estate agent."

Liv considered this for a second. She didn't claim to be any kind of genius, but unless she was missing something, dinner with a real estate agent could mean only one of two things. Either they were thinking about moving Nana somewhere new, or...

"They want to move?"

Nana nodded.

"Here?"

Another nod. "They wanted to consider it anyway. They wouldn't have done anything until after you'd graduated, but they wanted to check things out first, make sure it was even an option before they started talking about it seriously."

Liv said nothing. She guessed she couldn't blame them for wanting to gather information, and if moving would make them happy, who was she to stand in the way? Especially when she'd be away at school anyway. But why not tell her? She didn't like being left out of the loop. Never had. What did they think she'd do with that kind of information?

Throw a hissy fit like some dumb kid? She was practically an adult for crying out loud.

On the other hand, could she really be upset at them for keeping things to themselves when she'd been carrying around secrets of her own? Maybe there was no bigger waste of time than faulting people for being human.

"I guess that's what all the whispering was about."

"Whispering?" Nana glanced her way again.

Liv shook her head. "Never mind."

"It's not that they don't trust you," Nana said.

"Read minds much?"

Nana smiled. "They just didn't want to burden you if they didn't have to. It's a parent thing. Trust me. You'll understand someday if you have kids of your own."

"It's fine," Liv said. "Really." It wasn't, but they had bigger things to worry about. She'd forgotten about the monsters, if only for a second, but she knew they'd never be far from her thoughts. Not now, and probably not for the rest of her life. She unwrapped a second wet wipe and went back to work.

When they reached The Beachside, Connie parked around the far side of the structure. Liv had done a fair job of cleaning the muck off her face and out of her hair, but the stains on her clothing were probably permanent. She wasn't sure they could avoid attention completely even if they used the side entrance, but she knew the chances were better than if they marched in through the lobby.

Or she hoped so anyway. She wasn't sure she totally

trusted her judgment at the moment. Her mind was aflutter. She doubted she'd ever be able to reconcile what she'd experienced tonight with her long, otherwise-sane life.

She led Liv into the resort, scanning the hallway, ready to hide the girl behind herself if necessary, but the hall was empty.

As they crept toward the elevator like a couple of burglars, Liv still barefoot, Connie touched her left pocket. The bulge of the gun made her feel simultaneously reassured and guilty. She carried a room card in the same pocket. Had it been only hours earlier that Benji handed her the card in case she or Liv needed anything while he and Em were out? Was it really possible for such an integral period of your life to span less than a single day?

The elevator doors opened, and they stepped inside.

"Everything will be okay now," Connie said.

Liv looked at her, and Connie told herself she saw a sliver of hope in the girl's traumatized eyes.

Fred held the door for Agnes and followed her into the enormous lobby.

Festive music floated down from speakers hidden somewhere in the ceiling. The Christmas tree at the end of the space sparkled, and though Agnes didn't appear to give it a second glance, Fred paused to admire it. He'd seen plenty of Christmas trees over the years, some in the days when Christmas wasn't much more than a scattered, low-key oddity, but this one definitely ranked among the most beautiful.

Something about the complementary shades of silver and blue gave him a genuine sense of Christmas joy. Though he knew memories of this night would always include a mishmash of conflicting emotions, here was one thing he could look back on with pure fondness.

Agnes strode across the room, looking powerful and downright gorgeous in her rejuvenated body. A thin man in a half-decent suit smiled at her from behind the check-in desk. Fred jogged to catch up. Save for the three of them, the lobby was empty.

"Good evening," the man said. He had a nasally, affected accent and a snobbish face to match. His golden name tag reflected the lobby's overhead lights. DIGBY. "How may I help you tonight?"

"We're here to see my brother and his family," Agnes said. Her voice sounded pleasant enough, but after all this time, it wasn't hard for Fred to pick out the underlying tone of menace. He stopped just behind her.

"Of course," Digby said with a quick nod. "If you'll give me their names, I'll be happy to call their room and let them know you're here."

Agnes leaned forward and crossed her arms on the counter, probably doing a not-so-surreptitious job of showing off her cleavage, though Fred couldn't tell for sure from his position. "Actually," she said, "could you just tell us their room number? We want to surprise them."

Digby stiffened. "I'm sorry," he said, "but that would be against policy. I'm sure you understand."

"I do," Agnes said. She placed her hands palm down on the counter and vaulted over it effortlessly. Fred glanced around the room, checking to be sure no one else had wandered in.

Digby recoiled, clearly unprepared for this turn of events. "What..." he said. "You can't..."

Agnes grabbed a ballpoint pen from a mug behind the counter and swung it at the man's head with no further warning. The pen punctured his neck beside his Adam's apple. Its back half quivered while he gurgled and stared at her in shock. Instead of pulling the pen free, Agnes swung the flat of her hand into it, driving it the rest of the way into his throat and through his spinal column.

Fred had seen Agnes kill plenty of people, some of them in nearly the same way, but he'd never seen her do it with a pen. Adrenaline coursed through his body, and he felt himself begin to shift, but he pushed back against the urge. It wasn't time yet.

Digby dropped to the floor without another sound, instantly motionless. The force of the fall drove the pen back through the front of his neck. Blood oozed down the barrel.

"Hide his body," Agnes said. "We'll come back for it later."

While she moved to a computer and began poking at its keyboard, Fred walked around the desk, grabbed the dead man's arms, and dragged him through a doorway into a small, utilitarian office.

When he returned, Agnes patted his cheek and said, "Same last name. Room 312."

They walked away from the desk and past the Christmas tree. When Agnes called for the elevator, her thumb left a thin smear of blood on the button. Fred licked his lips and smiled.

While Nana called the police to update them on the situation and their current whereabouts, Liv found a plastic bag and filled it with ice from the freezer. She'd discovered a darkening bruise on her ribs where the monster hit her. Long and thin. It looked like someone had attacked her with a baseball bat. Her muscles throbbed, and every breath seemed more laborious than the last. She had little doubt she'd see the inside of a hospital room before the night was done.

Just don't let it be internal bleeding, she thought. *Or worse.*

She pressed the ice pack against her side and winced. She'd slipped into clean clothes and a pair of backup sneakers. While she waited for the ice to work its magic, she tapped her toes nervously.

Two dirty plates sat beside the sink, physical proof that her parents' lives carried on without her. For the first time, she seriously considered the future. Whether Mom and Dad moved down here or stayed back home, they had years of life left, and she wouldn't give them any grief about wanting to make the most of those years, despite the...what word had Mom used...subterfuge? No, she decided, she'd be totally magnanimous about the whole thing.

See, I know big words too.

Nana had moved to the bedroom, and though Liv could hear her, she couldn't make out most of what she was saying. Not that it really mattered. She knew what had happened.

Then again, maybe she *should* listen. Because she doubted Nana was giving them the whole story, and it would probably be best if they got their accounts straight. What was she supposed to say when they questioned her? The truth was crazy, but a lie might make her a suspect. She closed her eyes, turned her face to the ceiling, and sighed.

The knock seemed to come from somewhere far away—another room or maybe even another floor of the resort.

Liv opened her eyes.

More knocking. Louder this time.

She looked at the door and frowned.

Nana hadn't come back from the bedroom. It seemed like she'd been talking forever, and she sounded frustrated.

Another knock.

Liv got up, exhaling through a surge of pain, left the bag of ice on the counter, and walked to the door.

"Yes?" She pressed her eye to the peephole.

A couple stood just outside the door. They might have been about the same age as her parents or a few years younger, but she didn't recognize them.

"It's me," the man said.

The woman looked at him, and he shrugged.

"Me who?" She looked up to confirm the door's swing bar lock was engaged.

"Will you open the door? Please?"

For a second, Liv almost did exactly that, and if she hadn't been attacked once already that night, she might have. It was the *please* that did it. Politeness didn't negate trouble, of course, but try telling that to your instincts.

"No," Liv said and backed away from the door. "The police are already on their way here. Go away."

No response from the other side of the door.

For a second, Liv thought maybe they'd left. Maybe they had the wrong room. Maybe it had been a genuine misunderstanding.

And then something pounded against the door, rocking it in its frame.

Liv screamed and backed away several more steps.

Nana rushed into the room. "What—"

Another blow—a kick, Liv guessed—and the door rocked again.

The third kick did it. The swing bar snapped loose, and the door flew open. Chunks of drywall and a twisted length of metal framework exploded into the room.

The couple hurried in, scuttling through the doorway in an odd, unnatural way. When they moved farther into the room, Liv understood why.

They were changing.

While their limbs elongated and their torsos bulged, they stripped out of their clothing. Despite all the unbelievable, life-altering things Liv had seen today, this had to be the strangest sight yet. You haven't experienced true weirdness until you've seen a monster disrobe.

Liv moved to one side, putting distance between herself and Nana. The woman turned to Nana, and the man focused on Liv.

"Liv!" Nana shouted. "Run."

Liv looked at the ruined door. The creatures stood directly between it and Nana, but Liv might be able to make it out if—

The man, now almost entirely transformed, jumped at her.

Without thinking, Liv dropped and rolled beneath him. His feet slapped against the floor where she'd just been standing, but instead of looking back, she ran for the door.

She didn't want to leave Nana, but what else could she do? Maybe separating the creatures would improve their chances of getting away. What was it they said? Divide and conquer?

Except she and Nana were divided as well now, and she

had a gut-wrenching feeling they wouldn't be the ones doing the conquering.

Doors zipped past as she sprinted down the hall. She half-expected someone to poke a head out, curious about all the noise, but she saw no one.

She spotted the elevator ahead and knew there was absolutely no way she could stop and wait for it. The pursuing monster was right behind her—the sounds of its feet thwacking against the floor and its lanky limbs scraping the walls couldn't have been more than a few inches away.

From the room, she heard a gunshot and a meaty thunk.

Please let Nana be okay. Please.

Ignoring the twinges in her already-sore and overworked muscles, she raced past the elevator, heading for the stairwell to the lobby. Her new necklace bounced back and forth between her chest and the inside of her shirt. When she hit the stairwell door, she burst through it and down the first flight of concrete steps with no hesitation whatsoever. The creature entered the stairwell behind her and screeched. The sound bounced off the hard walls and steps, echoing through the space until it sounded like something prehistoric.

Liv didn't slow. She couldn't. If she slowed down, she'd die.

You might die anyway.

Yes, she guessed she probably *would*. But not without a fight.

The monster seemed to have issues with the stairs. She didn't look up, didn't want to risk disorienting herself and falling, but it sounded like it slipped down several steps and slammed into the wall. It screamed again, but this time there was irritation in the sound, and possibly even some pain.

That's wishful thinking.

Maybe its feet were too big for the treads or its body too disproportionate to maintain its balance on structures designed for human beings. Whatever the case, it gave Liv some kind of advantage, and she'd take whatever she could get.

She hurried down the stairs two at a time, huffing, thinking about her next move. If she reached the lobby, maybe there'd be someone there to help her, or somewhere to hide.

When she passed the door to the second floor, she pushed herself harder than ever. Just two more sets of stairs to go. Above, the creature slipped and roared again. Liv finally risked a quick glance in its direction and saw it staring at her over the railing. Its eyes were full of ruthless rage.

She reached the lobby door, hardly able to believe she'd made it this far, pushed through, and found herself surrounded by Christmas music and glittering decorations.

She scanned the room, still running and looking for anyone, but the space was completely empty. No guests. No staff. Nothing.

While she ran to the table in the center of the room where the resort had put out the complimentary snacks and an enormous dispenser of cucumber water, she looked for somewhere to go, somewhere to tuck herself away.

Behind her, the door to the stairwell flew open. The creature lunged into the lobby. Liv glanced back over her shoulder. The thing stopped, cocked its head, and smiled.

Liv would have given everything she'd ever owned to remove that smile from her memory. It made her want to roll up and cry. Or just kill herself before the beast could get its disgusting hands on her.

It ran for her, and though its legs looked too scrawny to hold up its body, they must have been deceptively powerful, because it moved with superhuman speed and agility. No cumbersome stairs to deal with now.

Liv ducked under the table, not knowing what else to do. When the creature leapt, it landed on the surface above her, knocking a tray of cookies and the water dispenser to the floor. The dispenser's lid flew off, and cucumber slices and snickerdoodles floated away in the rush of water.

The creature screamed again and rattled the table.

Liv had to get away. She was completely unprotected here —the monster needed only to curl its freakish arms around the edges of the tabletop to get at her.

She took a deep breath and charged out across the room. Her sneakers splashed through the spilled water. The enormous Christmas tree loomed ahead. She heard the table scoot across the floor and knew the monster had jumped again. At what she hoped was the last possible second, she zagged to her left and waited to feel a set of claws around her neck or the thing's meat-grinder of a mouth on her shoulder.

But it missed her. It hit the wet floor behind her and slid. When she looked back, she saw it skidding across the floor and into the tree.

The collision sent ornaments clattering to the ground. The creature spun, twisting itself up in a strand of lights and clawing at them viciously.

One of the ornaments rolled across the floor and struck the tip of Liv's sneaker. It was raindrop shaped and seemed to be made of metal. Its point looked dangerously sharp, and she wondered why they would decorate their tree with such a thing. Had they never heard of liability?

She looked from the ornament to the monster, which was still clamoring to untangle itself from the lights. Artificial tree limbs swished around its jerking body.

Attack now. While it's distracted.

It might be her best opportunity. Maybe her *only* opportunity.

She picked up the metallic object. It was heavy, solid. She gripped its bulbous end and let the pointed tip poke out through her fingers. Although she was completely aware that it might be the stupidest thing she'd ever done, she ran at the creature, raised the makeshift weapon, and lunged.

The monster saw the attack coming at the last second and tried to cover its face, but its arms were too thin to provide much shielding. The ornament swung through the gap between the limbs and pierced the thing's left eye.

It squealed, and dark vitreous fluid spilled down its face. Before it could retaliate, Liv swung the ornament again. This time, she hit it in its temple with a ferocious blow that sounded like a boot breaking through a sheet of ice. The ornament stuck fast, and when the monster wrenched away from her, it took the weapon with it.

Liv fell back on her hip, and the creature contorted further into the tree, clawing at the ornament lodged in its skull while more decorations rained down around it. Its loose skin came away in bloody strips when it raked its claws across its face. It finally managed to jerk Liv's weapon out of its head, but it was too late. It had already started to shrink back into its human form.

Liv crawled over to the convulsing thing. Its one good eye was full of hatred and terror.

"What *are* you?" Liv said, careful to stay just out of its reach.

The thing was now more man than monster. Most of the skin on the side of his face was torn away, revealing the wet, pulsing muscles beneath. The uninjured half of his head looked totally unexceptional—he could have been a cashier bagging her groceries or a math teacher finding the length of a hypotenuse. He pursed his lips, blew out a blood-pinkened bubble, and spat at Liv. The saliva came nowhere near her, but she flinched away anyway.

The man convulsed one last time, slumped, and stilled.

Liv found the bloody teardrop beside him, picked it up, and stabbed him with it three more times. Just to be sure. Once in the head, once in the neck, and once in the heart. She left the ornament there, protruding from his naked chest, stood, and backed away.

She walked through the spilled water, stepping indifferently on soggy cookies, and glanced around the room. Still empty. There should have been someone behind the desk to check in guests, right? Or a maid passing through? Someone? Hadn't all the noise drawn the attention of anyone?

The elevator dinged.

Liv stared at the metal doors and watched her distorted reflection slip away as the panels slid apart.

A half-transformed monster stumbled into the lobby. It held one hand against its ruined abdomen. Behind it, streaks of blood covered the elevator's floor and walls.

When it saw the body beside the tree, it raised its head like a wolf and howled.

Liv didn't back away this time.

She didn't need to.

The creature-woman stumbled first left and then right, spilling sheets of blood down her thickening legs. She spotted

Liv and tried to straighten her course, but she was able to take only one more step before dropping to a knee. She sucked in watery, ragged breaths and narrowed her nearly human eyes.

"You..." she said, and that was all. She flopped forward, striking the floor with a lifeless slap.

Liv watched the body, looking for movement, for any final signs of life, and saw nothing.

But she had to be sure. She grabbed a strand of lights from the tree, yanking it away from the limbs and out from under the first creature, and carried it to the second body. She looped the strand under the woman-thing's head, crossed it behind her neck, and pulled with all her remaining strength.

She pulled until her fingers were numb, until she could barely breathe from the effort. Then she dropped the lights, scooted away from the corpse, and screamed.

She sat between smears of spilled monster blood for several minutes, breathing heavily, before finally pushing herself to her feet and clomping to the elevator.

Nana had shot the creature, and Liv couldn't be prouder of her for that, but that didn't mean she wasn't hurt up there. Hurt or...

No, she wouldn't let herself think it.

The elevator's buttons were covered in blood. She pressed the 3, leaned her forehead against the wall, and waited for the machine to take her up.

Connie sat with her back against the wall beside the bedroom door. Blood oozed from her mangled arm, but rather than weakened or woozy, she felt invigorated, powerful. It made no sense.

Liv stumbled through the busted doorway, and for a second, Connie thought of that old movie she and Henry had watched all those years ago.

They're coming to get you, Barbra.

All the color had drained from the girl's face. Her eyes and cheeks looked hollow, malnourished, and she was once again covered in splatters of blood.

"Liv."

Liv turned to her, ran to her, and knelt at her side.

"You're alive," Liv said.

Connie nodded—then she shook her head. She looked down at her arm and remembered what the creature had done, the bizarre sensation of having her blood first sucked out and then forced back in, the terrifying sound of the thing's mouth working like some sort of organic transfusion machine while it tried to hold in its own guts and glared at her maliciously. Rows of bite marks arced away from her elbow, seeping blood, but they didn't hurt. Not like they should have.

She stared at her granddaughter. She saw the wonderful, smart, funny, generous, beautiful girl she loved with all her heart, but she also saw something deeper, something that both revolted and excited her, something...appetizing.

"Help will be here soon," Liv said. "Just hold on."

Connie shook her head and pushed away from the wall. When she tried to stand, Liv helped her to her feet, and it took significant willpower not to lean forward and take a bite out of the girl's over-worried face.

"We have to get out of here," Connie said. "I have to."

Liv told her the police were on the way, and probably am-
bulances too, but Connie couldn't wait for that. She was be-
coming...something else, and she wasn't sure how much
longer she'd have control of herself.

She bent forward, ignoring her creaking joints and burning muscles, and scooped the revolver off the floor.

One shot left.

"I'm going to the beach," she said. "I want to see the water.
You stay here."

"Are you crazy?" She shook her head. "You aren't going
anywhere without me."

"F...fine...you come too."

"I don't—"

"Please."

Liv's uncertainty was written all over her face, but she nodded and led Connie out of the room.

They moved, and Connie turned her head away from the
girl. She didn't want to smell her. She couldn't stand the
temptation.

They saw no one as they limped through the resort. Not in
the blood-soaked elevator or the corpse-ridden lobby, and
not by the pool when they exited the building. It was as if
they'd slipped into some parallel, uninhabited universe, and
though Liv relished the thought of not having to explain why
she was covered in blood, she also knew that if she didn't see
another human face soon, she might literally go insane.

After pushing through an iron gate, they walked down a

narrow path between patches of beach grass and stepped onto the sand.

There, finally, Liv saw actual human beings. A young couple sat near the water with their arms around each other, staring up into the star-filled sky and whispering. They didn't notice Liv and Nana, and that was just fine. It was enough to know they were there.

Nana held her hand and led her farther down the shore. The sound of the waves rolling toward them eased some of Liv's tension, but it wasn't enough to calm her completely. She wasn't sure she'd ever feel totally calm again. She kept remembering the sight of the creature clawing at its own face and the feel of the Christmas lights digging into her fingers as she strangled the naked woman-thing.

They passed an old man walking in the opposite direction, and though he probably could have seen them in the moonlight—well enough to see the state they were in at least—he gave them only a perfunctory nod, seemingly lost in thought.

They walked around a small dune, found an empty stretch of beach, and stopped. Waves rolled, and somewhere in the distance, sirens wailed.

"Liv?" Nana reached up, as if to stroke the side of her face, but then lowered her hand and took a big step back, toward the water. "I love you," she said.

Liv had heard the words a million times, but they seemed strange now, too out of the blue.

"What—"

"I'm sorry," Nana said. "They did something to me."

In the moonlight, she looked pale, almost ghostly.

"What do you mean?" Liv said. "Are—"

"I..." Nana hunched over slightly and made a sound that reminded Liv of a hissing cat. "I don't want to hurt you."

"Hurt me?"

Another wave ran over Nana's feet. Liv took a step forward. Nana took another step back. Her feet sank into the wet sand as the water receded.

"You'd never hurt me," Liv said. "What's wrong?"

"Tell my boys I love them. And your mom."

"You're scaring me," Liv said.

"And you. I love you so much. You've been the best part of my whole life."

"Nana—"

"I need you to close your eyes now, okay?" Her head twitched one way, then the other.

"No," Liv said. "Tell me what's happening."

"Please," Nana said. "For me. Please."

And although every instinct told her not to do it, Liv did.

The echoing sound of the gunshot nearly drowned out the splash that followed. When Liv opened her eyes, she saw her nana spilling blood into the flow of salt water that swept across what was left of her once-lively face.

The people came then. First the old man, and then the young couple, and then others. They came to see who was screaming...and why she wouldn't stop.

12

On Christmas Eve, Liv waited for the crosswalk signal and hurried across the road. A plow had just deposited a fresh bank of gray, litter-filled snow along the sidewalk. She hopped over the mush and lowered her head against the biting wind now blowing directly in her face.

Bundled-up pedestrians scurried down the sidewalk, exhaling plumes. Liv wove around them, flinching every time a passing car sent up a spray of icy sludge.

There'd been no word from Florida for days. The authorities had confiscated the resort's surveillance footage, and they'd kept her name away from the press. She had no doubt she'd have to face the music sooner or later, but her bigger fear right now was that she'd turn the next corner and find a black van full of government types with a bag for her head and a needle for her arm.

Just because it hadn't happened yet didn't mean it never would.

When she reached Andi's building, a doorman let her into the lobby and pulled the door shut behind her. Liv stopped and soaked in the room's warmth before moving on to the elevator.

While she rode up to the seventh floor, she touched the

bare skin of her neck and reached a hand into her pocket to confirm the gift-wrapped jewelry box was still there.

She heard the music before she reached the apartment. When she knocked, Andi's father opened the door.

"Liv!" Mr. Rigby said. "Merry Christmas."

Liv smiled and returned the sentiment.

The apartment was full of laughter and the smell of hot chocolate.

Mr. Rigby cupped a hand around the side of his mouth and leaned forward slightly. "I'm really glad you two are talking again," he said quietly.

"Me too."

He stepped aside and motioned her in with a theatrical swing of the arm. "Well, come on in. Our house is your house."

Liv entered the apartment, stripped off her outerwear, and went to find her friend. They had much to discuss, and though she hoped they had plenty of time to do it, you never really knew, did you?

13

O tis stood near the refreshment table with a cup of hot coffee, sipping the brew and watching his fellow retirees mill about.

When Mabel Piper walked over to talk to him, she touched his shoulder and shook her head. It was a combination of gestures he'd grown all too familiar with over the last few days.

"I'm so sorry to hear about your family," Mabel said. She wore a gaudy reindeer sweater and too much blush.

He nodded and thanked her.

"Those little boys were just the cutest things I'd ever seen. I've never seen twins so *identical*. It's so sad."

He said he agreed, it was very sad, and when she asked him how he was holding up, he gave her the same answer he gave everyone else: "I'm hanging in there."

"I just can't believe something like that could happen *here*."

"I know." As if there might be a place in the world where such things were run of the mill.

She asked if he thought it was all over, and he only shrugged. He genuinely had no idea.

After Mabel offered her final condolences and wandered

away, another woman approached him. She didn't touch his shoulder. She didn't shake her head.

"Come with me," she said and grabbed his arm.

She led him into a poorly lit hallway. Before he knew what was happening, she'd unbuttoned his cuff and rolled his sleeve up over the crook of his elbow.

"Hey," he said and tried to pull his arm away, but she was stronger than she looked and didn't let go. She grasped his bicep in one hand and his forearm in the other and leaned in close. He held the coffee in his other hand. Some of it sloshed over the rim, and he nearly dropped the cup.

"I thought so," she said.

The wound on his arm had started to heal, which was a miracle on its own—these days, it seemed any new cut, bruise, ache, or pain lingered indefinitely—but you could still clearly see the distinctive pattern: concentric circles spreading out from the elbow, each a series of dozens of pinpricks, now scabbed over but still inflamed and purplish. A lesion marked the center of the wound like a bullseye. The skin surrounding it was puffy and bright red.

"How do you feel?"

"I'm hanging in there," Otis said automatically.

"No." The woman shook her head. "How do you *feel*? Are you hungry?"

When she finally took her hands off his arm, Otis rolled down his sleeve. "I guess I could eat," he said.

The woman groaned. "I mean, are you craving flesh? Have you fed on anyone?" Her face tensed. She looked equally worried and furious.

Otis's heart rattled. "How did you—"

"Have you *fed*?"

He shook his head.

Some of her tension fell away. "Okay," she said, "good."

"Do you know what's happening to me?"

Now the woman grabbed his shoulder. Her fingers felt like steel. "Someone made a stupid mistake," she said. "That's what happened. And they didn't loop me in. Again."

He waited.

"But that doesn't matter now. They're gone, and we'll have to start over. Just the two of us. We'll have to move down the coast a ways—they ruined this place for us—but...I'm going to need you to do exactly what I say, okay?"

After only a short hesitation, Otis nodded.

"And if you do that," she said, "you'll live lifetimes upon lifetimes. How does that sound?"

He only stared.

"The most important thing," she said, "is that you can't feed. Not yet. We won't be ready for another cycle until next year."

"Next year?"

"Yes." She'd stopped looking at Otis and seemed to be lost in thought. "They come down every year. The snowbirds. Kids and grandkids and what-have-yous."

Otis frowned.

"We don't have to do anything. Do you understand? They come to us. We only have to wait here with our mouths open and be patient."

"I'm sorry," Otis said. "I have no idea what you're saying."

"I know," she said. She looked at him again, and it felt like she was staring right into his soul. "I'm going to explain everything. We have all the time in the world now, and we'll get through it together, but you have to promise me something."

"What?"

"Never leave me. We're a pack now. Whatever we do, we do it together. There were more of us, but they tried to do it on their own, and now they're dead. I don't want that for you. Or me."

"Okay," he said, "I promise." It was an easy promise to make. Although he wasn't entirely sure why, something about being near her felt *right*. Some kind of instinctual reaction he'd never experienced in his long, long life.

She brushed a strand of unnaturally dark hair from her forehead.

"Have we met before?" he asked.

"Not like this we haven't." She stuck out her hand. "Harriet Ikeda."

He shook her small, powerful hand and gave her his full name.

"For now," she said, "we need to go back in there and pretend everything is normal. Like we're just the same as the rest of them. Do you think you can do that?"

"I guess so."

She slapped his arm and said, "Don't worry, it's easier than you'd think."

He rebuttoned his cuff and followed her back to the refreshment table. Then he topped off his coffee and grinned. He'd never imagined that at the end of his life, things would just be beginning.

AFTERWORD

Several years ago, I wrote a collection of Christmas horror stories called Advent. The idea for the book was that you'd get one short story for every day of December leading up to Christmas, just like...well, you know...an advent calendar. This had been a passion project of mine for years, and it turned out even better than I'd hoped, but as much as I loved the stories, I thought the collection needed something more, something readers could really sink their teeth into, so I decided to include a bonus novella.

The book you just read was (and is) that novella.

Now, okay, I'm not sure if you're thinking that makes total sense or none at all, and I guess that's kind of the point.

Personally, I thought *Snowbirds* worked pretty well with the rest of my Christmas stories, and I love it exactly as is, but I knew even as I was writing it that it didn't really *need* to be a Christmas story. Like *Die Hard* and *Gremlins*, it takes places during the season and occasionally relies on festive elements to further the plot, but it probably could have happened any other time of year without losing too much of its overall je ne sais quoi.

Maybe I'm wrong about that, but I don't think so, because at its heart, *Snowbirds* is a monster story, and you and I both know monster season never ends...

And on that cheery note, whether it's snowing outside or sweltering, thank you for reading my book. I know time is a luxury, and I'm eternally grateful you spent some of yours lost in my wild imaginings. I hope you have a very happy whatever holiday is up next. But listen, seriously, if it's one of those things where your grandma or your grandpa or your elderly neighbor shows up for a visit, don't forget to lean in close and check for extra teeth...

DANIEL PYLE is the author of *Advent, Breakdown, Dismember,* and many other novellas and short stories. He is also the editor of *Unnatural Disasters.* After graduating from Amherst College, he moved back home to Springfield, Missouri, where he now lives with his wife and three children. Visit him at danielpyle.com.